OUTDONE!

Rourke advanced. The assassin he'd targeted was ready to fire on another group of defenseless people. Rourke stepped away from the wall, the Centennial in his right hand at near full extension. He drew the trigger back until the cylinder was fully rotated and was just ready to break. *"Hey!"*

When the assassin wheeled toward him, Rourke pulled the trigger that extra fraction of an inch. The little stainless steel .38 bucked hard under the pressure of the Plus P load. The bridge of the killer's nose collapsed, blood spurting from his face as he fell back.

It was only then that Rourke felt the cold barrel of a weapon at the base of his skull.

"How convenient of you to come, Mr. Rourke. I'm glad we can finally meet."

THE SURVIVALIST SERIES
by Jerry Ahern

#21

THE SURVIVALIST

...TO END ALL WAR

BY JERRY AHERN

ZEBRA BOOKS
KENSINGTON PUBLISHING CORP.

ZEBRA BOOKS

are published by

Kensington Publishing Corp.
475 Park Avenue South
New York, NY 10016

First printing: October, 1990

Printed in the United States of America

For our old friend Tom Conrad of Taurus, who tells us he likes reading Ahern books; hope you like this one, buddy. . . .

Any resemblance . . .

Chapter One

Fiery fingers hissed above the high mountain plateau, groping upward into the night's icy blackness. Cadaverous hulks of twisted steel and titanium alloys were at the base of each towering plume of flame, glowing brightly in the burning synth fuel that, moments earlier, had powered the mighty Soviet war machines. But now the Russian armor, like once fearsome prehistoric beasts, lay dismembered, sprawling and inert.

For a moment only, John Rourke remembered Natalia's uncle, Ismael Varakov, commanding general of the Soviet North American Army of Occupation, and his office without walls in the museum in Chicago so very long ago. Dominating the center of the museum floor were the reconstructed skeletons of two massive beasts, now extinct.

The fires formed a wall, seemingly impenetrable, a flickering, yellow-orange artificial horizon. And they surrounded John Rourke, Michael Rourke, and Paul Rubenstein.

Thick trailers of blue smoke raced over the snow-packed rock and debris-strewn landscape on heat-fed frigid winds. Everywhere, blemishing and pockmarking its fire-tinted whiteness, were bits of burning wreckage, ranging in size from the minute to the immense, nearly all that remained now of the armada of T-91 tanks, armored personnel carriers, and the battleship-sized mobile missile-launching platforms all, that is, except for their glowing skeletons.

John Rourke, a thin, dark tobacco cigar clamped in his teeth, moved his right hand. It hurt badly from the burns he'd sustained from the live steam, bleeding in some spots where the skin had cracked. He thrust it back into a side pocket of his parka.

And he was cold, colder than he could ever remember having been.

Flames of Rourke's own creation, necessary to burn an escape hole through the Plexiglas-like substance that armored the gunner's dome of a Soviet missile-launching platform, had nearly devoured him. The flames had burned away large portions of his arctic gear, despite the clothing's fire-retardant protection. But the drifts he'd plunged into, when jumping clear of the huge machine as it rolled over the edge of the great plateau, had extinguished the flames. The out-of-control missile platform rolled and tumbled, destroying itself as it plummeted into the abyss beyond. Rourke burrowed into the snow to save himself from incineration, obtaining what protection he could as the other enemy machines around him exploded, targeted by the missiles from the mobile launcher he had just evacuated.

As the snow melted into icy water, it permeated the linings of his parka and snowpants, saturating his arctic gear and the sweater and battle dress utilities beneath. And now the wetness was penetrating to his skin, causing him to shiver almost uncontrollably. Each second that elapsed chilled the dampness into ice. Progressively, his body temperature was dropping. Rourke's medical training and his common sense told him that he must find shelter, must strip off his refreezing garments before hypothermia set in hard enough to kill.

John Rourke had a design change in mind for the German winter gear. Since fire was such a hazard under arctic conditions, the clothing could be made to self-fuse to a mid layer, thus being self-sealing over the lining, affording at least some protection to the wearer from direct exposure to harsh temperatures after the flames were extinguished.

He made a mental note to mention these proposed design modifications for cold weather gear to the engineers of New Germany in Argentina.

But now, staying alive was the more urgent matter. He

threw away the cigar. Smoking would only further compound his body's attempts to normalize temperature in any event.

Rourke reached for the energy weapon he had risked his life to obtain. But Paul was already picking it up from the snow beside Rourke's feet. "Come on," John Rourke shouted over the crackling of flames, the howling of the wind. And, orienting himself, he started into a jog trot toward the German armored vehicle he had dubbed "Atsack," the massive machine barely visible against the snowfield as an odd-shaped mound, the synth-fuel fires burning dangerously close to it.

Paul and Michael fell in on either side of him, Rourke calling out to his son, "Did you turn the systems back on?" If Michael had not, the Atsack would only be a windbreak, but otherwise nearly as cold as the natural environment surrounding them.

"Everything's up and ready. And, with enough speed up, we can roll through those fires without burning the treads," Michael shouted, realizing that his father's hearing would be impaired for a while longer, at least.

Rourke knew that, only nodding now. The double exertion of running and shivering was beginning to tax strength that was already depleted as a result of the battle to take control of the Soviet missile platform and to capture the coveted energy weapon. As they neared the mounded snow, the outline of the Atsack took on greater definition. The full-treated, all-terrain vehicle was taller than a single-story house from the days Before the Night of the War, the wedge-shaped titanium plow taller than any man, reminiscent of the cowcatchers on the nineteenth-century steam locomotives that had once plied the western frontier.

The Atsack's rear access was closed, as it should be. Rourke pulled his right hand from his pocket, using it more for balance than for anything else, most of his right glove having been burned away in any event. To have touched the bare metal would have cost him more skin.

And he climbed now, up the tread and toward the portside ladder, shuffling snow from the rungs as he moved, gingerly sliding his flame-burned left hand along the vertical stanchion.

He reached the height of the Atsack's superstructure, tugging at the hatch, throwing it back. Desperation and exhaustion drove him, powered him, Rourke knew. Paul and Michael, navigating the Soviet energy weapon between them as they climbed, were just below him, mounting the superstructure. The energy weapon was about the size of a prewar M60 machine gun, and about the same heaviness. Paul had it now as Rourke started down through the hatchway, into the air-locking chemically, biologically, and radiologically sealed antechamber. Michael slid down the ladder's verticals, jumping to the floor just behind Rourke.

The energy weapon was being passed down, Michael taking it, then Paul coming down the ladder, not so rapidly but quickly enough. As Paul passed beyond the hatch, he slung it back. Rourke hit the powered locking unit controls, the hatch securing.

Then John Rourke activated the air scrubbers.

Air—seemingly cold, despite its obviously greater warmth than its exterior counterpart—flooded the compartment with a roar. Rourke swallowed to equalize the mounting pressure in his ears.

Finally, the green light indicator flashed on.

Rourke activated the interior hatch controls. There was a pneumatic sigh, then the hatchway opened.

John Rourke started downward and through, the comparative warmth suffocating to him.

He dropped the rest of the way down the ladder and into the Atsack's ready room. As he crossed out of the way of the ladder base, he unbuckled the black leather gunbelt at his waist, snaking it, together with the .44 Magnum revolver and LS-X survival/fighting knife, to the surface of a bulkhead-mounted three-man-wide seat.

Immediately, Rourke dropped to his knees, clumsily

stripping his arctic parka from his body with his burned hands. With his left hand, he drew first one, then the other of his Scoremasters from his trouser band, setting the gleaming stainless steel .45's beside his gunbelt. His sweater, like a prewar Woolie-Pulley, was heavy with half-frozen water.

Rourke tore away the snow goggles that hung around his neck, then pulled off the toque that covered his head and threw it down. And, at last, he removed his sweater.

He tugged the little Smith & Wesson 9mm with the suppressor and slide lock free of his clothes, placing the pistol on the seat.

Michael was in the ready room, taking the captured energy weapon from Paul, who was coming down the ladder after him. Paul jumped the last few rungs, skinning out of his parka and goggles, still wearing his toque and snow pants. He bit off his outer gloves, grabbing down the self-heating thermal-insulated blankets from the racks on the opposite bulkhead. "We'll have you warm, John!"

Rourke rasped, "The hell with it," but not to his friend. He drew the little A.G. Russell Sting IA Black Chrome from its sheath just inside the waistband of his trousers, running one edge along the expendable laces of his boots, severing them rather them untying them. He put the knife down beside the other weapons as he kicked free of his boots.

Already, his left hand was tearing open the burn-tattered snow pants. His BDUs beneath them were soaked in melted snow. Rourke pushed the snow pants down, then the BDUs, dropping to the floor in his underpants. Michael kneeled down beside his father, grabbing the snow pants by the bottoms of the legs and pulling on them. "When you were a kid, I'd undress you for bed sometimes," John Rourke told his son. "Never quite — quite this hurriedly." Rourke's teeth were chattering.

As Michael started on the BDU pants, Paul was there, taking the double Alessi shoulder rig from Rourke's body, then helping his friend's progressively shakier fingers with

11

the buttons at the top of his black knit shirt. Rourke tugged the shirt upward and off, Paul throwing one of the blankets around the man's shoulders and back, rubbing him with it to dry him, to warm him.

The blanket used natural electric currents within the body to power its heating elements—an electric blanket that never needed plugging in.

Michael pulled off Rourke's socks, taking up a second blanket and throwing it over his father's legs, wrapping it around them. "I'll microwave coffee." As Michael stripped away his parka, he exited the ready room.

Paul changed the blankets on Rourke's upper body, wrapping another one tightly around his friend. "Keep that closed. How you doin'?"

"Freezing. Fine."

The younger man only nodded, starting to massage Rourke's legs and feet. "Any numbness?"

"No. I'm just—just so—" John Rourke's concentration was going. He only wanted to sleep.

As if Paul somehow understood that, Rourke's friend shouted to him, "No sleep until we get some warm fluids into you. Right?"

John Rourke barely nodded, barely whispered, "Right."

Paul changed the blanket on Rourke's legs. "Michael! Get in here!"

Rourke fought to keep his eyes open, exhausted from shivering, forcing himself to . . . And then Michael and Paul were on either side of him, chair lifting him between them, holding the blankets around him. Michael ducked John Rourke's head as they crossed through the bulkhead door into the Atsack's main compartment. They placed him on one of the lower fold-out crew bunks, wrapping the blankets tightly around him. Already, the blankets were starting to heat up. Paul elevated Rourke's head, while Michael held the cup of coffee to his father's lips. "It's hot, but not too hot to drink."

Rourke tried to nod. He sipped at the coffee, letting it wash down his throat, feeling it burning inside him.

"Drink it all and then sleep," Paul ordered.

Rourke drank more of the coffee, thinking maybe then they'd let him close his eyes.

The blankets were quite warm now, and even though he was still shaking with the cold, he told himself everything would be all right—if only they'd let him sleep.

Chapter Two

Some called it a sixth sense.

Natalia Anastasia Tiemerovna, Major, Committee for State Security of the Soviet (Retired), didn't know what it was called. But in times like these, she had it; and, when in the past she'd ignored it, she'd at least been lucky enough to live to regret it rather than not living at all.

Annie signaled a stop, saying, "I've got to adjust this strap."

Natalia nodded, easing down her half of the improvised travois they'd made, upon which lay the likely dying German officer they'd rescued. The man and his gutted helicopter had been bait to draw her and the other women out of The Retreat, into the hands of Freidrich Rausch, the brother of Damien Rausch, whom Sarah Rourke had killed.

The neo-Nazi personnel who had waited for them, sucking them into the trap with the plaintive messages from a dying aviator, had almost been too easy to kill, Natalia told herself.

And none of them had been Freidrich Rausch.

Of that, she was certain, because Freidrich Rausch would not have been easy to kill at all. Rausch had eluded John Rourke, and that in itself said something quite considerable about the man.

So, where was Rausch?

The answer, she realized, as she adjusted her parka hood against the snow, which seemed to fall unendingly, and against the wind, which roared over the lonely road they struggled up toward The Retreat, was that Freidrich Rausch was watching them. She knew it in her bones, in her soul.

That was the sixth sense impression she felt.

And the dilemma Rausch's presence presented was a clear one.

If, with Annie helping her, they brought the critically in-

14

jured young German officer back to The Retreat, Rausch would at last know The Retreat's precise location and, worse yet, the location of its primary entrance.

If they did not bring the man inside, the young helicopter pilot would surely die. And, if they waited outside, they would eventually die, too. As a matter of course, she and Annie had brought emergency rations, as well as a good supply of ammunition, and were dressed for temperatures even lower than what they now experienced.

They could survive several days, especially if they erected a shelter or found some natural rock formation that would serve as a windbreak.

But, what then?

"You're worried," Annie said over the keening of the wind.

"You're right. Are you reading me?"

"Right now, anybody could read your mind, Natalia."

Natalia rubbed her gloved hands together. "He is our problem, this poor man. I think we are being observed by more of the Nazis, perhaps Freidrich Rausch himself."

"I've felt someone watching us," Annie said. "But we can't let him die." She gestured to the young man on the travois.

Natalia nodded. John always triumphed through reasoned daring. "Are you up to a climb?"

Annie pulled down her snow goggles. "What do you mean?"

"I have an idea." Natalia dropped to her knees in the snow, checking the young man for a pulse and finding one, but barely.

If he'd been dead, their options would have been greater, but human life was of more concern to her than expediency. And, as she stood, she caught up her piece of harness on the travois. Annie repositioned her goggles and did the same.

"We have to hurry," Natalia said. As she spoke, she pulled her scarf closer over her mouth and started hauling on the harness again.

The road leading to The Retreat had never seemed as steep to her as it did now, nor as long. The windchill was something she could only guess at, but it had definitely increased since they'd left the warmth of John's Retreat to trace the mysterious radio message. Sarah and Maria Leuden, the lover of Michael Rourke, would be anxious for them now, of course, the time factor considerably more protracted than had been predicted.

As they continued along the road toward The Retreat, Natalia silently wondered if this time she might be gambling too much, because if she lost, not only would she lose The Retreat, but all of their lives as well. . . .

Hugo Goerdler rubbed his double-gloved, none-the-less cold hands together. The rocks behind which he and Freidrich Rausch now hid served as a moderately effective windbreak, but not effective enough. He was chilled to the bone.

Rausch held infrared binoculars to his eyes, peering down over the lower portion of the rock wall toward the road across the wide chasm and somewhat below them. Along the road, the two women who had defeated Rausch's team of men still moved, towing after them a litter on which was the body of the helicopter pilot whom they had used as bait to draw the women out.

"Soon, Goerdler. They will have to enter the mountain hideaway soon. Then, we have them."

"Have them," Goerdler mentally echoed. He was reasonably convinced that the women would have been a better choice to aid him in achieving his goals . . . better than Rausch and his bully boys.

"And what then, after we have them, Freidrich?" Goerdler finally asked him.

Rausch, without shifting his gaze, still looking through the binoculars, said, "I have the explosives ready with which to blast our way inside, and then I will summon the remainder of my force. We detonate, invade the facility, and Rourke's wife will die. His daughter and the other two women will be held hostage for Rourke's cooperation in our plans. Success."

Hugo Goerdler admitted to himself that Rausch's plan sounded very simple and very effective, but whether or not it could be accomplished was another question. . . .

Natalia stood guard at the outer Retreat door until Sarah and Maria helped Annie get the near-death pilot inside. Natalia abandoned the closed door now, racing through the red lit chamber between the outer and inner doors, then through the vaultlike inner doorway. Annie and Sarah hauled the inner door closed, securing the locking system.

Natalia tugged off her gloves, pushed down her hood, and started unwinding her head scarves as she went to the electronics console. John Rourke's external security system for The Retreat had recently been upgraded with state-of-the-art German technology. Before she even sat down, she started summoning up on the various closed circuit screens vision-intensified video images of the area immediately surrounding The Retreat.

She stripped off her gunbelt that held the two L-Frame Smith & Wessons, opened her parka, and undid the bib front of her snow pants, letting them fall to her waist.

As Natalia shifted from one video source to the next on the main screen, she picked up movement, then changed video sources for the secondary and tertiary screens and began manipulating direction controls on the three cameras that were trained on the same spot. "Come here, Annie," Natalia called out.

As background noise, below her level of concentration, she could hear Sarah, an experienced nurse, telling Maria what she needed. Natalia considered the young pilot's chances for survival nearly zero, but they had to try to save him nonetheless.

In a moment, Annie was behind her, looking over her shoulder. Natalia glanced at her, then turned away. "Those two men. They were watching us, of course, and from their vantage point, they could certainly see The Retreat entrance. I doubt they could tell there's the inner door, but even so, we're compromised."

"I'm ready when you are."

17

Natalia nodded, saying, "He'll use explosives, if that's Freidrich Rausch. And I'm sure it is. Explosives and a backup team, but this time his good people, not the ones he sent against us before. Get one of your father's sniper rifles for me . . . ammunition for it. Take some grenades."

"And rope," Annie almost whispered.

"Yes, plenty of rope."

Chapter Three

Annie and Natalia left the Great Room, entering the principal storage room (although there were other storage areas within and below The Retreat). Here even greater quantities of ammunition than before were stored, because John Rourke had recently restocked with fresh supplies fabricated for him by the Germans. John had always, ever since Natalia had first met him, displayed a marked preference for one brand of ammunition and only one, that from Federal Cartridge Company. Now, he had so successfully induced the engineers of New Germany to duplicate the Federal loads for his firearms — 185-grain JHP for .45 ACP, 180-grain JHP for .44 Magnum, 115-grain JHP for those few chores he deemed best served by a 9mm, etc. — that the Germans had even reproduced the familiar red and white boxes to the last detail.

In addition to the ammunition, of course, there was a wealth of material.

There were crates of everything, from feminine hygiene necessities, to synthetic motor oil, to dehydrated freeze-dried foods, holsters, gas masks and bags, gas mask filters, state-of-the-art German cold weather gear, German chemical-biological-radiological protective suits, cleaning supplies for everything from kitchen countertops to firearms, spare parts, hoses, and belts for every piece of motorized equipment in The Retreat, from the hydroelectric generators that powered it to the videotape machines. Replacements for items that could not be readily repaired were held in storage, ready to be brought on line.

Natalia wondered what John was getting ready for. She looked toward Annie.

The two of them crossed the room, set down their arctic parkas, and put their combined weight and strength against

19

the high-rise metal tool cabinet, moving it aside but barely able to do so.

Behind the tool cabinet was a steel door, three feet square, a combination lock on it. Natalia deferred to Annie, who put her hand to the dial and turned it right, then left, then right. She put her left hand to the handle, twisted, and the door swung open.

Natalia shouldered into her coat, picked up the Steyr-Mannlicher SSG, and leaned it against the wall. Then she fetched a large metal tool box, placed it under the door, stepped up on it, and pulled herself into the crawl space of the exit tunnel, a mini flashlight clamped in her teeth. She smiled, realizing that she'd just applied lipstick and would leave it on the tube of the flashlight. Annie passed her up to the SSG and musette bag of ammunition, then called softly from behind her, "I'm with you."

She crawled toward the first rung, the rungs anchored into the living granite three feet apart from one another. The diffused light through the door behind her suddenly died as Annie slammed it shut. Natalia turned her head, aiming the flashlight in her teeth toward her friend's right hand as Annie moved the interior combination dial, locking the door.

Natalia looked ahead and upward, the tunnel angling steeply toward the summit of the mountain. Annie behind her, she began to climb. The solitary beam of light from the flashlight she held clamped between her teeth swayed left to right as she alternated hands and feet on the evenly spaced rungs. At last, weary of the weight of the rifle and her other weapons, warm in the heavy German arctic gear, she reached the second door.

Not combination locked, it was otherwise identical to the door in The Retreat wall that was covered by the high-rise tool cabinet. There was a steel bar, heavy-looking, lying across it. Both the door and the frame around it were fitted with heavy synth-rubber gaskets, newly replaced when John had gone through The Retreat substituting anything that could possibly be wearing out or deteriorating. She balanced herself on the rungs, pushing, pushing harder, finally dislodging the bar.

The door was harder to dislodge, the seal between the rubber gaskets like a powerful suction. But, at last, she was able to wrench it open.

Beyond, in the beam of her flashlight, was more of the upthrusting tunnel, the rungs three feet apart. She pushed her way through the doorway and began to climb, looking back once. In the wavering light, she could see Annie, struggling through the opening in her heavy clothes, with her burdens.

As Natalia continued the climb, she could hear Annie behind her now, closing the door.

At last, Natalia stopped at the third door. Like the intermediate door, it was only sealed with a bar and surrounded by heavy synth-rubber gaskets. But surrounding the doorway were wires, all connected to a plastic and metal unit roughly the size of a package of cigarettes.

John had placed the new alarm on the outermost door. Routinely, rather than bothering Sarah and Elaine below, Natalia disabled the high-tech unit, then used her muscle power against the bar.

It moved. She shifted it aside.

Annie was close beside her now. As Natalia wrenched open the door, she was greeted by a faceful of icy cold snow. And Annie laughed.

Chapter Four

Michael drove the Atsack, while his father slept from a mild sedative cocktail he had administered to him, the elder Rourke's hands bandaged and treated with some of the new ointment from the doctors at Mid-Wake, even a more powerful healing agent (although less conveniently administered and non-antiseptic) than the German spray that had become part of their standard equipment.

And Paul Rubenstein entered in his journal, "We have just done what under normal circumstances, viewed objectively, I would have considered impossible—again. For a time, I thought that this time we would surely not make it, that never again would I be with my wife, John's daughter, Annie.

"Times like these, when there is quiet and no imminent danger, are the times I miss her the most, times when I can think.

"So, now we have an all-but-operational sample of the Soviet particle beam energy weapon. Coupled with the plans brought to us by the KGB Elite Corps officer Vassily Prokopiev, we should have the means by which to duplicate this awesome weapon.

"And, I have mixed feelings concerning that. Is introduction of a new weapon of wholesale slaughter to mankind's ultimate advantage? Objectively, of course not. But, subjectively, we have no choice. The Russians of the Underground City, once they have united with their counterparts beneath the sea, the historic enemies of Mid-Wake these past five centuries, will have nuclear capabilities and platforms from which to launch the enormous Soviet submarines known as Island Classers. To prevent ourselves from being overrun and being forced to utilize the still-experimental nuclear weapons the Germans are fabricating to counter the Russian threat, we must achieve parity on the battlefield and turn that parity to superiority.

"Why did Nicolai Antonovitch, the commander of the combined armies of the Underground City and the forces which served under Karamatsov, dispatch Prokopiev to us in the first place? Obviously, he trusted the young officer. Indeed, Prokopiev proved himself an honorable man (and probably sealed his fate at the same time) when he assisted us at the battle for the Second Chinese City, helping us to neutralize the nuclear warhead missile the Chinese of the Second City were about to launch as part of some religious ritual which still terrifies me just to think of it.

"But, why?

"Antonovitch must realize that the planet cannot endure a second thermonuclear confrontation. His superiors in the hierarchy of the Underground City do not realize that.

"He values the fate of human kind above ambition. Bless him.

"I feel that very soon this seemingly endless battle will conclude, one way or the other. Annie and I have decided wisely to wait before having children. I sometimes worry very much for the child John gave Sarah that she still carries to term. Will the child die before birth, in a final war?

"Or will the child be born to a world of peace and freedom?

"I hope that it will, and that soon after it the first child of Annie and myself will join it in that new world. But the threat of what lies before us is so great that sometimes that peaceful time is beyond my imagining.

"How, if that world comes, will I support my wife? I was a young editor at a trade magazine Before the Night of The War, the very night I met John Rourke. I have lived many lifetimes of danger since then. Could I return to electronics or writing, or any 'normal' occupation in this new world? Or would I die, instead, of boredom?

"At least, Annie and I will be together, in death, in life, in whatever the future holds. Despite all my regrets, lost friends and family, and places I held dear destroyed in the bombings the Night of the War or in the Great Conflagration, when the atmosphere caught fire and nearly destroyed all life, some things I will never regret are the love which arose between Annie and me, my friendship with Michael Rourke, with Natalia, with Sarah, all the others—and, most especially, John Thomas Rourke.

"I know him well enough to understand and forgive his solitary weakness, yet never so well that I do not marvel at his strengths. His weakness is his perfection. He is more than other men, and he pays the price for that. He is my friend. There could be no greater honor than that."

Paul Rubenstein looked up from his journal and stared at the Atsack's bulkhead wall. After a time, he shifted his gaze, focusing on the sleeping form of John Rourke. High forehead, but naturally so, a full shock of dark brown hair just touched with gray, both a face and physique that were at the least imposing.

"Perfect," Rubenstein smiled.

Chapter Five

Annie said, "You should be the last one down, because you're the best shot." The wind blew with incredible force here atop the mountain, her father's mountain. "That way, you can cover me with Daddy's rifle."

Natalia looked at her, saying nothing for a moment, then nodding. "All right, but—"

Annie smiled beneath the scarves that swathed her face, beneath the snorkel hood of the German arctic parka. "—But be careful?"

"Something like that, Annie."

Annie Rourke Rubenstein tied onto the rope, weaving it to the figure eight descender on the Swiss-Seat-style rappelling harness she wore. She checked the harness where it met the D-rings, tugging at it in every conceivable direction. After her father, John Rourke, had awakened from The Sleep, he'd spent five years with Annie and her older brother, by two years, Michael, educating them in survival. Rappelling was one of the things she had never liked but had been forced to learn . . . and learn well.

As she started toward the edge of the small, flat expanse at the summit, Annie remembered those days. "Why do I have to learn something like rappelling, Daddy? I'm a girl!"

"Up until comparatively recently in human history, being a girl meant you weren't taught to read and write . . . weren't allowed to vote in an election . . . in some areas weren't even allowed to own property. Being born a girl meant that you were property. But, let me ask you something."

"What?"

Her father had smiled, a little bit embarrassed-looking. "Aside from peeing standing up without getting his legs wet, what can a boy do that you can't?"

25

"Daddy!"

"Men have greater upper body strength, but women have a greater threshold of pain; and, even though they're more sensitive to temperature variances, women can withstand greater temperature extremes. Women tend to be more verbal, while men tend to be more analytical. Yet that didn't seem to hamper great female scientists such as Marie Curie or great female philosophers such as Ayn Rand, did it?"

"No."

"So, just because you're a girl now and someday you'll be a grown woman doesn't mean you can't learn anything . . . do anything . . . accomplish anything a boy can do who'll someday grow to be a man, right?"

She'd thought about that for a moment, then looked at him and nodded.

"So, get your little butt over to that rope and shout down to your brother to belay it before you start down."

And she'd done just that, getting her little butt over to the rope, locking on, shouting down to her brother and, after a lot of embarrassing failures, getting pretty good at it — as good as her brother, as a matter of fact.

In those days, she'd still been learning that if her father was going to take the time to teach her something, it was because he knew she could excel at it if she tried.

John Rourke was not now and had never been, to her memory, a man who wasted time on useless endeavors.

"Keep me covered, Natalia," Annie called out, then jumped, controlling her descent, halting it, both feet going against the rock wall, kicking out, then descending again. If the Nazis under this Freidrich Rausch were watching this near side of the mountain rather than the main entrance to The Retreat, she might very likely be dead before she reached the base.

Again she kicked off, gliding downward. Slung to her back was an M16. Belted around her waist were her two usual handguns, the Detonics Scoremaster .45 and the Beretta 92F, but there was also a third handgun this time, a fixed sight Taurus 9mm 92 AF, cosmetically almost identical to the Beretta but with three major differences: The safety system was of the type where the pistol could be carried cocked and locked or hammer down; it was satin chromed; and anchored beneath the forward portion of the frame was a Laser Aim LA1. Zeroed to the weapon upon which it was mounted, it might prove valuable in the darkness.

And that was why she'd taken it from the arms lockers.

The Taurus was loose in one of the several musette bags slung across her torso, shoulder to hip.

Again, Annie kicked out, continuing to descend.

Snow swirled around her, the winds near the base of the mountain even stronger. She was cold, oh so cold, but told herself that the sooner this was over the sooner she'd be able to take a hot shower, wash her hair, slip into a gown and robe.

Despite all the training, rappelling still mildly terrified her, and Annie realized that was one of the reasons she was cold now.

She kicked off again, descending more slowly now, the base of the mountain near.

She sank chest deep into a drift, then sagged back, hauling on the rope and pulling her way along the base of the mountain, through the drift, at last breaking free of it and sinking to her knees.

There was no sign of the enemy.

She freed herself of the rope, gave it three rapid tugs, waited a second, then tugged three times again.

Under different circumstances, she would have belayed the lines to ease Natalia's descent, but under different circumstances, Annie wouldn't have been rappelling down the side of the mountain in the first place. Covering Natalia's descent was more important.

For that purpose, Annie extracted the laser-sighted Taurus semi-automatic from the musette bag in which she'd carried it. Its fifteen-round magazines were not interchangeable with those of the Beretta, although her father had once told her they could be altered for that purpose. But the four spare magazines she carried were not so altered.

Annie tugged down her snorkel hood a little, pushed down the scarf covering her mouth, and bit off the outer glove on her

27

right hand. With only the silk glove liner beneath, she had nearly full tactile abilities. She linked the two plugs that connected the battery-operated laser tube to the control switch. Had she done so earlier, she would needlessly have depleted the reserve. And, at best, she had about thirty-two minutes of actual use before recharging would be necessary. Thirty-two minutes could be enough time for hundreds of shots, because the laser only bled power when the switch was actually activated. But, as her father had taught her, there was no sense in not planning ahead.

The coupling completed, Annie press-checked the Taurus, edging the slide back just enough to visually confirm a chambered round, never trusting memory or indicators or anything else other than her own senses.

The Taurus was chambered loaded, giving her sixteen rounds ready.

She tested the laser with a brief flash into the snowdrift near her, its red dot almost comfortingly warm to her. Then she eased her second finger against the pressure-sensitive switch.

And Annie moved ahead, along the base of the mountain, searching for a position of concealment and cover from which she could simultaneously protect Natalia and herself.

She found a niche of rock and moved into it, letting the snow bury her to the waist. With her snow-smock covering the arctic parka, she should be all but invisible, she hoped, and the rocks would provide cover from enemy fire from three sides.

She crouched there, a loose grip on the laser-sighted Taurus 9mm, her eyes straining for a glimpse of Natalia descending along the rock face. . . .

Natalia Anastasia Tiemerovna, both a Steyr-Mannlicher SSG and an M16 slung to her back, both on cross body slings, descended rapidly along the mountainside, her goggled eyes scanning below her, trying to penetrate the cyclonically swirling snow.

There were no sounds of gunfire, nothing to indicate that Annie had been detected in her descent moments earlier. And

Annie was remarkably good.

In the days Before the Night of the War, as well as afterward, when she'd worked actively in the KGB, there were always the jokes about the so-called talented amateurs of popular fiction. But Annie, although it was hard to ever consider her an amateur, was truly that. Natalia would have staked her life on Annie's courage and skills as willingly as on one of the talents of the most highly trained professional in the KGB, the Mossad, the British SIS, the American CIA, or any other organization.

She had her father's intuitiveness for doing just the right thing at just the right time, along with a woman's lateral approach to head-on confrontation. Annie Rourke Rubenstein was the ideal agent or officer, even though she'd never actually been one. Emotional, open, feminine, none of these qualities interfering whatsoever with Annie's abilities to tackle the job at hand and emerge victorious, in fact, these attributes only served to enhance her abilities.

Natalia kicked away, controlling her descent, her right hand ready to leave the rope and grab for one of the twin L-Frame Smith & Wesson revolvers holstered at her right hip.

The guns. She thought about them for the first time in a long time. They had been a gift from revolversmith Ron Mahovsky, to the man who succeeded to the presidency of the United States. President Chambers had awarded them to her after the collaborative effort between United States and Soviet personnel to evacuate peninsular Florida

He'd told her that, as an American president, he could not award a medal — even had he access to one — to an enemy agent. So he'd given her the revolvers instead.

The barrels were flattened along the sides, and the right ones were engraved "American Eagles."

She'd used them for steady carry in the field ever after that, in the holsters that accompanied them, on a belt John had found for her that would more properly fit her woman's waist.

She kicked off, nearing the ground she was sure.

And there was still no sign of fighting below. . . .

* * *

29

From her vantage point, when she craned her neck just so, Annie could see the rock in front of The Retreat entrance, which had to be moved in order to open the outer door. And, beside it now, oblivious to the possibility — fact — that surveillance cameras could be monitoring their every move, were two men.

But, in the distance, when there was a moment's lull in the icy north wind, she heard the soft whisper of silenced rotor blades . . . a German gunship.

Annie did not delude herself.

Help was not forthcoming.

If the Nazis had stolen one gunship and its pilot to serve their nefarious ends, they could just as easily have stolen two or three. Coming through the night would be Nazi reinforcements.

The two men beside the rock seemed to be doing something other than lurking about. She saw a cylindrically shaped metallic object that could have been an explosive charge, likely was. Annie bit her lower lip beneath the scarf that protected her mouth from the snow and the cold. The gunship might have missile capabilities . . . in all likelihood would have such capabilities. Certainly, the missiles coupled with an explosive charge could penetrate through the outer door. The interior vault door was another matter, of heavy-gauge steel. But an explosive charge — a second one — might damage it enough that entry could be gained.

"Damn," Annie hissed under her breath.

Rausch, most certainly one of the men on the ground, could have given compass coordinates to his men aboard the chopper, but most likely was bringing them in by transponder or merely by ordinary modern radio.

If she could kill Rausch and the man with him, whoever he might be, Annie might be able to confuse the helicopter into landing either farther away or off the road entirely, crashing. But, in either event, she must keep The Retreat entrance a secret from the Nazis. Otherwise, whatever she did to Rausch and the man with him would only be a temporary respite.

So, there were only seconds.

She glanced once toward the face of the mountain.

Natalia was visible as a shadow within a swirl of snow, still some thirty to forty-five seconds from touching down.

There was no time to wait.

Annie Rourke Rubenstein left the cover and concealment of the rocks, starting forward, all but swimming through the deeply drifted snow, keeping the muzzle of the laser-sighted Taurus up above it.

She had no worry about the M16, its muzzle cap in place. And, again, she remembered the words of her father during those five years he had so intensely educated and trained them. "What do you call this thing on the muzzle of my CAR-15 again?"

"A muzzle cap?"

"Now, look at this." They'd been standing in the main supply room, and he'd taken down a rather large box, opened it, and turned it at an angle so that when she stood on her tiptoes she could look inside. The box was full to the brim with more of the muzzle caps that fitted tight over the flash hider and, she already knew, blocked entry of dirt, water, or other foreign material through the muzzle end of the barrel. "What do you see?"

"A whole bunch of them."

"Right. So, whenever you need to protect the bore of your weapon, use one of these. But, whenever you might need a shot very fast, don't worry about shooting through it, because I've got enough to last us for a very long time. Okay, Annie?"

"Okay," Annie had told him.

The M16's chamber was loaded. All she needed to do, if the pistol proved insufficient for the task, was to swing the assault rifle forward, flick the tumbler from safe to auto, and pull the trigger.

There was an extra muzzle cap in the same bag in which she carried spare magazines for the M16.

She kept moving. . . .

As Natalia kicked away from the rock wall, there was a lull in the wind and she heard the unmistakable sound of a silenced

German helicopter gunship in the night.

"Damn," she hissed under her breath.

It was like the sound of a fly buzzing in one's room in the darkness, distinct, annoying, recognizable. With all the time she'd spent working with Vladmir Karamatsov on behalf of KGB interests in Latin America, the sound of a fly buzzing in a room was nothing strange to Natalia.

If the Nazis had commandeered one of the German military gunships for the purposes of drawing them — the women — out of The Retreat, it was logical to assume that they could have commandeered a second or third gunship as well. Evaluating the situation empirically, she could arrive at no other more likely conclusion than the gunship being manned by Nazis having come to reinforce Freidrich Rausch in his intended assault against The Retreat's main entrance.

Natalia let herself descend more rapidly than was wise, nearly more rapidly than was prudent toward the drifted-over ground below. . . .

Annie was as close as she dared without being detected.

She checked the laser again, shining it into the snow.

Her father had taught her many things, some of which she'd recalled tonight. One thing he had told her in those five years when, for all they knew, the lives in The Retreat were the only lives on Earth, she remembered now. "If you are ever placed in the position of having to take human life — and God only knows, we might be the only people left on Earth — remember this: If the necessity for taking life cannot be avoided, you must determine the morality of striking first. In other words, if you're good enough and willing to risk your life, then give your adversary a chance. But, even if you are good enough, and more than your own fate hangs in the balance, don't masturbate your honor or your conscience — and who's to say they aren't the same, really — but don't do that by sacrificing lives that may depend on yours to give a known enemy a so-called 'even break.' Usually, if an enemy is worth killing, he's worth killing by whatever means necessary to achieve the end result of his death and the preservation of your life or what other lives may depend on your success. So, if you have to, shooting a man in the back is just about the same as shooting a man in the front; the important consideration is not that he deserves to die, usually, but that the event of his death will achieve the desired result. If the result is worth killing for to begin with, the direction from which the bullet or knife or whatever comes that ends his life is largely immaterial. Do you understand, Annie?"

She hadn't understood then, because in the videotapes of western movies, the good guys never ever shot the bad guys when their backs were turned.

But she'd come to understand juxtaposing the values of lives, determining which was better, a troubled conscience or wasting the lives of the good and the innocent.

So Annie Rourke Rubenstein settled the laser-fitted pistol in her right fist, sitting back on her hind end. She spread her legs apart in a way that was unnatural for her because she so rarely wore slacks or pants. With her back propped against a snow-packed rock, her elbows rested just inside her thighs. She brought her left hand up, pulled back the hammer on the pistol, thumbed up the safety.

She forced her shoulders to relax, taking control of her breathing.

She could see both men through a niche of rock about eighteen inches wide.

The taller, brawnier of the two men was doing something with the cannister, which was likely some explosive device. The soft whirring of the helicopter rotor blades was louder now, almost audible between the lulls in the driving cold wind.

She moved her right thumb to just over the pad, which was the switch for the laser.

Her left thumb moved down the pistol's safety.

She wrapped her double-gloved left hand over her single-gloved right, around the front strap of the 9mm pistol.

Her right thumb depressed the switch for the laser, and the red dot appeared between the shoulder blades of the man with the supposed explosive device.

She let out half her breath, catching the rest in her throat,

33

blinked once, then touched her right first finger to the trigger.

He was already pitched forward, as if she'd hit him with a vastly heavier caliber than 9mm. Either she'd hit him in the spine, or . . .

The pistol bucked and the laser beam danced a zigzag pattern across the man's back and neck as she brought the gun down, swinging her entire body a few degrees right, firing again as she settled the laser beam over the juncture of the second man's neck and shoulder. He was already turning toward the sound of the first shot as she fired.

Again, the pistol rocked a little, the laser zigzagging.

She fired once more on the second man as she brought the pistol down, the laser beam just below his thorax as his body spun away.

She thought she'd hit high and off center because of the speed with which his head was turning away from her, possibly striking him in the jaw.

She swung the pistol toward the first man.

But he was gone.

"Damnit," Annie snapped. She moved the laser beam onto the second man again. His body was still, but she couldn't afford to leave him alive with the first one still in motion. She fired twice more into his thorax and head, killing him for certain.

As she triggered the second shot, she realized her error.

As she brought the pistol out of its mild recoil from that shot, she was already starting to move.

Either she'd hit the first man in the spine, or . . .

Whatever it was that had hit her on the side of the head made Annie's entire body vibrate with the impact and she sprawled right, barely holding onto the Taurus as she fell.

And then there was tremendous pressure on her, and there was a knife beside her left eye and a voice saying, "I will make you ugly before I kill you, Frau!"

Chapter Six

Natalia threw herself into the snow at the sound of the first shot, the icy wind rendering her unable to exactly peg the direction from which it had come.

The subsequent shots gave her her bearings.

And they were clearly just pistol shots, likely 9mms.

Annie had the laser-sighted Taurus from the arms lockers. If she'd had the opportunity to take out both men spotted earlier on the microwave closed circuit video monitors, she would have taken it, in all probability having elected to use the pistol.

The helicopter was much louder now, likely homing in on an open radio frequency. The road leading up to The Retreat became almost level for a short span, perhaps five hundred yards away from the entrance.

A skilled helicopter pilot could land there, even in those conditions.

But Annie would have been on the radio by now, announcing her success if she'd had any. Or she would have called out by voice to her.

But there had been no such radio transmission and no such call.

Natalia told herself she'd waited long enough, that she should have never put Annie in a position where the girl might have to brace someone her own father had so far been unable to best.

Natalia reached into the right side pocket of her parka, extracting the Bali-Song. She wedged the knife, still folded closed, inside the fold-around tab that secured the buckle of her gunbelt to the belt itself. Blousing up her parka slightly, she was able to mask its presence there from casual observation.

Swinging the M16 forward off her back, she clenched her right fist around the pistol grip, her right thumb poised over the selector for a split second.

The helicopter would land within minutes or less.

There was almost no time.

She flicked the tumbler to auto. Then, with her right first finger just outside the trigger guard, she started out of the snowdrift to find Annie and Freidrich Rausch. . . .

It was Freidrich Rausch. He said to her, "You are the daughter, are you not?"

Her eyes flickered from the point of the knife, less than an inch away from her left eye, to his face, and then back. His eyes were darkly gleaming pinpoints of light seen through his snow goggles. "I shot you," Annie whispered, trying to keep her voice steady.

"I was bending over and, as luck would have it — good luck for me and bad for you — the bullet tore away part of my parka but did not harm me at all. You are the daughter of Frau Rourke, the one who fornicates with the subhuman."

Annie moved her right hand, still holding the gun, and Rausch almost drove the knife through her snow goggles and into her eye. She sucked in her breath and froze, not daring to even breathe. He kept the knife so close to her eye that it actually touched her snow goggles as he reached out with his left hand and took the Taurus from her grasp.

"You are the Rourke daughter?"

"Yes."

"And you chose to despoil your own body by —"

"Fuck off! Understand that in English?!" He was going to kill her anyway, she realized.

Rausch laughed. "My men will be here. They will not be happy. You have just cold-bloodedly murdered one of the top officials in the party."

"Nazis eat shit three times a day," Annie hissed through the scarf covering her lips.

"And what if I blind you in both eyes and set you off somewhere in this icy wilderness to wander about in darkness and anguish and pain?"

"Better than your company," Annie told him honestly.

Rausch laughed. "How did you escape the mountain fortress of your father without being detected?"

She had the distinct impression that he hadn't seen Natalia. Annie fought to keep her expression fixed, not to show any relief, even in her eyes. "I won't tell you."

"We could blind you in one eye first, and of course my men are very lonely. If you will let this Jew lie with you—"

"You'd better kill me, because if you don't—"

He stabbed the point of the knife through the left lens of Annie's snow goggles, and she screamed as she reached to her belt for the Detonics Scoremaster .45 to kill him.

Natalia's voice rang out across the snow. "Hold it! Or I shoot!"

Annie lay still.

Her left eye was squinted tightly shut and she told herself she could feel the tip of Rausch's blade against the lid. Tears were forming involuntarily in her eyes. The fingertips of her right hand were on the butt of the .45.

She'd never make it.

Rausch smiled as Annie looked at him with her right eye. "Major Tiemerovna, the Communist agent. Welcome!"

"Major, not anymore. Communist, not anymore, either. Move and you will surely die."

"I think not, Fräulein Major! If you do not move into my line of sight and carefully lay down your weapons, I drive the knife forward, through her eye and into her brain. It is strong enough steel for that. And, if you shoot me, I will fall toward her and you will have done my work for me."

"Kill him!" Annie screamed.

But she didn't move.

"All right," Natalia said.

Annie wanted to shake her head in disbelief, to scream, to kill Rausch herself. She didn't move.

She could barely see Natalia, edging around on Rausch's left, lowering the muzzle of her M16. "Natalia!"

"I have no choice but to do what I must do, Annie!"

Rausch laughed again. "Keep coming, Fräulein Major.

37

And be quick about it."

Natalia kept moving, letting the muzzle of the M16 all the way down.

Finally, Rausch ordered, "Stop there!"

Natalia stopped.

Rausch commanded her, "Drop onto your knees, Fräulein Major."

Natalia obeyed.

Annie was too frightened to breathe.

Rausch said, "Gently let the rifle fall to your side."

Natalia obeyed.

"Now, easily, so there is no chance that I will have to kill the Jew lover yet. Unsling your weapons and let them fall beside you."

Natalia began to comply.

Annie's body shook with cold and rage. Her head ached, her muscles felt tied in knots. Out of the far corner of her right eye, she could watch Natalia clearly.

Rausch commanded, "Now the gunbelt, and very slowly."

Natalia began to unbuckle it, then shouted, "Fall back!"

Annie threw her body weight rearward, her right eye never leaving Natalia's hands. Natalia's right hand flew outward to full extension of her arm and something gleaming left her fingertips.

Annie felt downward, outward pressure on her goggles and twisted her head back and left.

As she turned away fully, she saw the knife as it plunged into Rausch's chest.

Annie's gun was out, firing point-blank as she heard a simultaneous shot, then another and another, from where Natalia still knelt.

Annie touched her snow goggles, ripping them from her face.

She opened her left eye.

Natalia trudged forward, her gunbelt over her left shoulder, her long guns still in the snow.

Annie started to cry, angry with herself for it but knowing it was a release of tension. And she remembered the words of her father: "Women generally live longer than men because

38

their emotions are closer to the surface, less bottled-up; never be ashamed to cry." And, something else he'd said: "There were eight people in the United States who could throw a Philippine Bali-Song knife while closed and have it impact the target open; but when Natalia first came here, that made nine."

Chapter Seven

Annie secured the dead Freidrich Rausch's snow goggles over her eyes, saying, "Daddy would have enjoyed watching you, I think."

Natalia smiled. "Don't make such a big thing out of my getting Rausch. The circumstances were just right, that's all. Your father would have done it at least as well, if not better."

Annie said nothing more about it, except, "Thank you."

"Friends never have to say that, but it is very nice when they do."

"I think they may have placed an explosive device near the main entrance." Natalia only nodded, strapping on her gunbelt, fetching up the sniper rifle and the Colt M16, running as rapidly as she could through the drifted snow toward the main entrance and the large rock before it. As Natalia bent over the metallic cylinder, Annie was beside her. "That's what I meant. It looks like—"

"It is." There was a timer, Natalia examining it in as minute detail as circumstances allowed. "I can't disarm this. So, we can either get it as far away from here as possible in—" And she looked away from the timer, turning to Annie. "We have four minutes and sixteen seconds."

"Or what?"

"We can give it back to the Nazis."

"I'd have to deliver it in person, wouldn't I?" And Annie smiled, the smile deceptively gentle when Natalia considered what her friend must be thinking. "All right."

Natalia double-checked the device, making as certain as she could that it was not rigged with some sort of gyroscopic contraption that would cause it to detonate when moved. In the end, it was a gamble, but she moved it and the timer didn't instantly accelerate, nor did the device explode in her hands.

They moved together along the side of the road, away from The Retreat, looking for a first glimpse of the German gunship that would be bringing more of the Nazis. As they took cover, they saw it.

The helicopter was touching down, skidding in almost elliptically toward the road. Annie and Natalia crouched in the rocks together, waiting for touchdown. "When I open fire and draw them off toward me, you'll have about thirty seconds. Run out there and get the device as close to the gunship as you dare, then get to cover. You'll need a good hundred yards to be safe, if we want to do it this way. More distance would be better and you'll need cover."

The sound of gunfire and the accompanying muzzle flashes would certainly have alerted the occupants that there was trouble in store. Natalia worked quickly with the Steyr-Mannlicher SSG, before the enemy gunship took action with which she could not deal. Because of the heavily falling, wind-swirling snow, the SSG's 3 X 9 variable scope's objective lens would instantly cover. She flipped up the switchlike lever both forward and rearward on the base, the levers locking the base to the milled rails at the top of the receiver. She slid the entire assembly forward and off, handing it to Annie.

Annie took the scope, securing it in one of the musette bags she wore. Then she picked up the bomb that now lay between them in the snow.

Nearly two and one-half minutes remained on the timer, Natalia knew, watching Annie for a second longer, then bringing the butt of the SSG to her right shoulder and squinting through her snow goggles along the simple iron sights. She speed-cocked the bolt, chambering the top round out of the five-shot rotary magazine.

The helicopter was down, men starting to pile out. In the next instant, Natalia snapped off the set trigger, then rested her right first finger just beside the trigger guard. "Ready?"

"Two minutes left on the timer. I'm ready."

"All right." Natalia barely touched the forward trigger. In the cold, crisp air, the sound of the .308 was an earsplitting

41

crack, and the SSG rocked against her shoulder as one of the snow-smock-clad Nazi personnel took the hit and tumbled back into the chopper's fuselage.

Natalia already had the bolt cocked, fired, killing another of the men, cocked, fired a third time, felling a third man. Then she dropped the rifle in the snow as she called to Annie, "Be ready!"

Natalia ran along the side of the road, away from The Retreat, firing the M16 that was slung to her side, keeping to short bursts, just long enough to attract the attention of the men from the helicopter. Gunfire hammered into the rocks near her, furrowing the snow. . . .

Annie was moving the instant Natalia dropped the SSG into the snow, the bomb — with a little under ninety seconds remaining on the counter — ticking in her hands. She ran back along the side of the roadbed, at first in the direction of The Retreat, glancing over her shoulder every chance she had, watching as Natalia drew off the personnel from the commandeered German helicopter.

The wild card in the thing, she knew, was that the helicopter might go airborne, in pursuit of Natalia. If it did, her gambit of using the bomb against the machine would prove impossible and she'd be forced to pitch the bomb over into the defile paralleling the road.

As she half stumbled through a drift, her eyes were riveted on the timer. Only seventy-four seconds remained until detonation.

She could no longer see Natalia as she stood up, and there was no time to look for her.

The bomb under her left arm, like she'd seen men carry a football in videos at The Retreat, Annie broke for the road, well away from the helicopter's personnel now, many of whom were on foot, chasing Natalia, a few standing perhaps twenty-five yards distant from the machine, as if not quite knowing what to do.

Annie ran, which was difficult to do with the heavy snow. Raising her feet high enough to move at all was a challenge, the exertion telling on her before she'd gone half the distance

42

she needed to go.

Sixty-three seconds on the timer.

"Football," Annie panted.

She ran, shifting the laser-sighted Taurus from her right hand to her belt, hefting the bomb.

It was heavy, but not inordinately so.

And every step she didn't have to take to deposit the bomb was a step she wouldn't have to take to escape its blast. There was always the chance that if the bomb were hurled and received a strong enough jar, it might detonate prematurely, but the snow was soft and she was running out of time.

Fifty-five seconds.

The bomb in her hands, the helicopter fifty yards away.

Annie ran, hauling her right arm back, her left hand still supporting the device as she drew her right hand level with her shoulder. She'd never paid that much attention to the football videos, but throwing was throwing, Annie reassured herself.

And she pivoted on her left foot, nearly losing her balance, hurtling the bomb toward the helicopter gunship.

Her right arm felt as if it were almost jerked from the shoulder socket. She turned, stumbling, catching herself, running now through the drifted snow covering the road, trying to retrace her original footprints as much as possible so she would have easier going.

She couldn't glance back.

There wasn't time.

But she counted seconds in her head. . . .

Natalia threw herself down into the drifted-over rocks, hauled the M16 up, and fired out the last few rounds in the magazine.

As she fired, she saw Annie running.

To herself, Natalia had been counting the seconds.

She was finished counting.

It the next instant the explosion came, starting about fifteen to twenty meters from the German gunship, a fireball, yellow and black with an orange corona gushing skyward and outward in all directions.

Natalia saw Annie running, then throwing her body over the rocks at the side of the road and down into the drifts.

The fireball grew, rolling outward, the helicopter seeming to start moving but too late, the fireball engulfing it. And, suddenly, there was a second explosion, even louder than the first, and a fireball even greater than before, belching upward on a column of black smoke, the helicopter consumed.

Natalia chambered the top round out of the fresh magazine in her M16 and opened fire on the Nazi personnel, some of them standing in the roadbed merely staring, some of them running, none of them thinking about the fleeing figure they'd been chasing seconds earlier, she knew.

And gunfire came from the edge of the roadbed . . . Annie.

Natalia took one of the grenades from the musette bag she carried and yanked out the pin, hurling it toward the men clustered between her position and the all-but-incinerated helicopter.

As the first grenade exploded, Natalia pulled the pin from a second one, threw it, then brought her M16 to her shoulder again.

The Nazis from the gunship did little more than abortively try to run for their lives, then die.

Chapter Eight

He loved his best friend like a son or brother, and loved his son like a brother or best friend. Each had become the other yet was still unique, an individual.

He was the most fortunate of men, John Rourke realized. His eyes were still closed but he was awake now, summoning strength to be fully so, at the same time assessing his body's condition. He felt weary in bone and muscle, but otherwise unimpaired. And the weariness would pass.

There was the smell of food cooking. He corrected himself—cooked. Aboard the Atsack, everything was microwaved, hence never a smell until it left its preparation medium. Like the coffee aboard the submarine vessels of Mid-Wake, the coffee here was made in its own microwave device. The food packets—vastly better-tasting and more nutritious five-centuries-removed counterparts of the old G.I. M.R.E (Meal, Ready to Eat)—were individually microwaved in units resembling large toasters, the side of the unit folding open instead of popping up when completed.

"Dad?"

Michael. John Rourke opened his eyes.

"Could you use something to eat?"

John Rourke didn't ask his son their tactical position. He assumed Paul was at the Atsack's controls and that, already, they had gotten well away from the site of their battle with the Soviet-armored missile unit. He wanted to urinate, but the smell of the food was somehow more urgent. "Yeah. You can stop yelling, Michael. My hearing seems to have returned to normal."

"Great. Let me help you sit up."

Rourke let Michael assist him. "I'm a little woozy."

"I gave you a very mild muscle relaxant/sedative cocktail

45

by injection. You've been asleep for three hours."

John Rourke shook his head, exhaling slowly. He took the packet—which had become rigid during the cooking process, forming its lower side into a bowl—and peeled the spork off the side, tasting the food—beef stew—and realizing his mouth was dry, cottony-tasting. "Give me something to drink, huh?"

"Right." John Rourke leaned back into the bulkhead as Michael went toward the service console. "Coffee?"

"Water."

"Right." Michael foot-pedaled the cold water spigot, filling a cup. As he brought it back, he said, "We're well away from any Soviet activity, best we can tell. Paul and I agreed that radio silence would be a good bet, so we haven't contacted Captain Hartmann's forces yet."

Rourke's son took the meal, exchanging it for the water. Rourke drank the water. Now he had to urinate. "I'll be right back."

"Stay off your feet. Wait." Michael took the cup, set down the meal on a small foldout table about the size of a Thompson chair desktop, and went off. John Rourke leaned his head back, closing his eyes. When he opened them, Michael was back, in his hand a disposable unit into which his father could urinate.

John Rourke took it, fumbled his way under the blankets swathing him, used it, sealed it, then handed it back. Michael took it back and went off to the disposal. John Rourke took his food from the small foldout table and tasted it again.

Microwaved food still lost its warmth quickly, but it was hot enough. He ate hungrily as Michael rejoined him. "After you get a shower, once you feel up to it, then maybe we can put our heads together and figure out our next step."

Through a mouthful of stew, Rourke told his son, "You and Paul seem to have things pretty well in hand." He swallowed. "We have to get somewhere where we can contact Hartmann's command for evacuation of the energy weapon by air, without bringing the Russians down on us first."

"Paul and I were talking, Dad. The Russians won't know

we've got this, will they?"

The thought had crossed Rourke's mind, too. If the energy weapon could be duplicated by utilizing the in-the-flesh article along with the plans Vassily Prokopiev had brought them at the behest of Antonovitch, there might be a onetime surprise use advantage. Antonovitch's motives, as Rourke understood them, were clear, however convoluted bringing them into reality might be; the Soviet military commander, one of the survivors from Karamatsov's pre-Night of the War KGB Elite Corps, had realized that another nuclear confrontation was in the offing unless he could give the allies pitted against the Soviet Underground City—the Americans of Mid-Wake, the surviving Icelandics, the First City Chinese, and the Germans—the means by which to achieve parity in the field without resorting to theater nuclear weapons.

"What are you thinking about, Dad?"

Rourke looked at his son and smiled. He was still a little fuzzy from the sleep and the sedative. "You were too young to remember then. But before the Night of the War, there was a strong move afoot in the Soviet Union toward democratization and toward stepping down from a war footing. Then things got out of hand, as you know. I was thinking about Antonovitch, how possibly he's lived to regret what the KGB Elite Corps did behind the scenes to bring about the war. Maybe he's thinking that preventing a final round of nuclear destruction is worth the price."

"Price?"

Rourke nodded, putting down his food on the little foldout table. "He'd rather have the Soviet Underground City lose this war than win it and destroy the entire planet for good this time."

Chapter Nine

Sarah Rourke sat with her hands cupped around her swelling abdomen. Her arms formed something reminiscent of a collapsed ballet bubble, she thought.

Maria exited the room in which the young helicopter pilot was resting, a grim look on her beautiful face. Annie asked, "How is — ?" But then, Sarah realized, it was as if Annie already knew.

Natalia said it. "Dead?"

Annie bit her lower lip, nodding. "So young."

"Wars are fought with the young, Annie, remember?" Sarah volunteered. She stood up from the couch, her back aching, the palms of her hands pressing against her kidneys as she straightened up.

Annie wore one of her ankle-length robes, the pink one, a dark blue towel turbanned over her hair. She sat down on the steps that lead from the bedroom she shared with Natalia and into the Great Room. "I'll get dressed. We need to bury him."

Natalia, her boots off but otherwise still attired for battle, lit a cigarette. She said, "We cannot stay here any longer. We were very fortunate this time that we were able to kill them all. Good luck is never something to be counted upon. If we remain at The Retreat, there will be other Nazis sent after us perhaps. Originally, Sarah, Rausch wanted to kill you because you killed his brother. But now, Annie and I have killed Rausch, and Annie recounted that Rausch told her she had killed a man who was very high up in their party.

"He was stupid or conceited enough to be carrying his party identification card on his body, and we found it when we searched him. His name was Hugo Goerdler."

Maria Leuden, sitting on the couch, took off her glasses and began to speak, her voice low. "Hugo Goerdler is —

was — one of the top-ranking men in the Party. He was prominent in the Youth, prominent under The Leader, likely was more prominent among the hard-liners. They will be after his killers."

"We will be in no greater or lesser danger if we rejoin John and Paul and Michael," Natalia said. "I vote that we leave here."

Sarah stood and leaned against the wall. She looked very tired. "I think we were pushed into this; I thought that from the beginning. Sometimes, I guess, it's very nice to feel protected, but we have a duty just the same as the men have. And I don't even feel like saying something cute about men getting in trouble without us there to keep them out of it."

Annie stood up, rearranging her robe. "If things come to a head, we should be where we can do the most good. I agree with Natalia that we won't be any safer here. And if Daddy and Paul and Michael are in danger, we don't have any right to try to keep ourselves out of everything just because we're women."

Natalia exhaled smoke, saying in almost a whisper, "A lot of this was because of me. But I learned out there that I'm back, like I was. Whether that's for good or for bad, I'm not any more or less likely to crack up than I would have been before what happened to me happened."

"Hen party's over, then," Sarah Rourke declared, feeling as if a burden had suddenly been lifted from her spirit.

Chapter Ten

The aircraft—a J7-V—came in almost diagonally over the pad near the main entrance of the mountain city that was the heart of New Germany in Argentina. And then it stopped.

It hovered as its engines changed orientation, then began to descend.

John Rourke looked below them.

A granite jewel in the midst of a verdant subtropical paradise, the mountain islands inside which lay the German city rose from the center of a garden landscape. But, unlike other times when Rourke had come here, no children played in the parklike grounds, no women in soft print dresses strolled after them, no scholarly-looking young men walked deep in thought.

Anti-aircraft missile batteries were set about the grounds instead, and all around were armored vehicles of every description from within the German inventory.

At each of the four corners of the pad onto which the J7-V was now settling were tanks, and surrounding each tank were infantry personnel.

Some distance back, well away from the aircraft, Rourke saw horse-mounted Long Range Mountain Patrol personnel, the men and the animals they rode all but lost inside the shade of the single canopy jungle that surrounded the park.

There was a gentle lurch and the J7-V was landed. John Rourke checked the bandages over his hands . . . lighter, barely necessary now except to protect the wounds there. New skin was already beginning to form and, most importantly, he could flex his fingers, hold a gun without opening the wounds and making them bleed again.

After getting the Atsack to a safe-enough location to risk rendezvous with Captain Hartmann's forces in the field, they had flown directly to the field headquarters. News of the possibility of obtaining the Soviet weapon had already spread to New Germany and scientific teams were even at that moment preparing.

Two days were consumed with carefully dismantling the weapon for every conceivable form of photography, analysis, and data recording. Once the photos, X-rays, computer blueprints, and other data were assembled and the weapon itself was reassembled, it was dispatched to New Germany, along with the original copy of the materials sent to them from the Underground City's military commander via the exiled Vassily Prokopiev.

Rourke spent several hours each of those two days undergoing skin grafts to his left hand, the grafted skin sooner to heal than the skin that had been scalded away.

Gratefully now, the J7-V landed, Rourke stood. The skin had been taken from the rear of his left thigh and he was still tender there.

Copies of the accumulated data were dispatched to New Germany by various other flights, over various routes, so that at least the data would certainly arrive in good order, even if something were to befall the Soviet weapon itself.

Two more days had been spent in travel, stopping first at Lydveldid Island to confer with Madame Jokli and her staff concerning the latest developments in the war; and, of course, to renew the friendship held by the entire Rourke family for Bjorn Rolvaag. The Icelandic policeman asked to accompany them to the fighting. Rourke conveyed to Rolvaag as best he could that they were on their way back from the active front in Eastern Europe to New Germany. But Rolvaag accompanied them in any event. They continued on to near Eden Base, where the women were waiting for them. Although he questioned the wisdom of their leaving The Retreat, he would be glad to have their help and, on one level at least, felt more at ease if they were near . . .

51

that if something occurred to endanger them, he would be there rather than unknowing and thousands of miles away.

John Rourke could not escape the feeling that things were now coming to a head, a climax. As to the outcome, he could not predict.

Michael walked aft from the J7-V's cockpit, announcing, "I just got off the radio. They want us inside quick. One of the Long Range Mountain Patrols reports Soviet troop movement toward the seacoast. There's some thought to the effect that the Soviets of the Underground City might have already affected their alliance with their counterparts near Mid-Wake and some sort of seaborne attack might be in the offing."

John Rourke took one of the thin, dark tobacco cigars from the pocket of the faded blue shirt he wore beneath his battered brown bomber jacket. He rolled it across his teeth, settling it unlit at the left corner of his mouth. "If the alliance is already working, going inside might not help much." Then he started toward the fuselage door. Paul was already opening it, and when the almost uncomfortably bright sunlight washed into the cabin, Rourke squinted against it. There were German military personnel waiting, an honor guard with assault rifles at order arms, and other military personnel as well, from among the number of these latter several assisting the rest of the way with the egress steps. Rourke reached to one of the patch pockets of his jacket, extracting the dark-lensed aviator sunglasses he hadn't needed very much in the blizzardlike conditions to the north. He needed them now.

He moved onto the steps, his pack in his right hand. One of the German junior officers reached for it and Rourke let him take it. An M16 was secured to the pack, Rourke's gunbelt was slung over his left shoulder.

From behind him, Paul said, "God it's bright out here!"

Rourke reached into his jeans, took the battered zippo from his pocket, and rolled the striking wheel under his right thumb, thrusting the tip of the cigar into the lighter's blue-yellow flame. He inhaled.

The main entrance to the city lay before them, armored vehicles nearly blocking it and positioned to do so rapidly. The blast doors were half closed. More than five times the usual number of guards were stationed there. Just on the exterior side of the entrance stood a military band.

Despite the dark-lensed glasses John Rourke wore, when he looked upward, he squinted against the light. From the air, as the J7-V made its approach, he had detected little additional fortification of the German city. But, from ground level, able to see beneath the overhangs that were blasted or laser cut into the mountain's exterior, the city's level of preparedness seemed considerably heightened. Anti-aircraft and anti-armor missiles were located at regular intervals on three levels, and logic dictated that the armament totally surround the mountain in a staggered tier effect.

Michael and Paul flanked him now.

The band began to play, striking up "The Star-Spangled Banner" as the commander of the honor guard formed on either side of Rourke, his son and his friend calling the unit to present arms.

Striding toward the aircraft from the edge of the landing field, with several junior officers and a number of civilian official-looking men in tow, was Col. Wolfgang Mann.

Colonel Mann, supreme military commander of the armed forces of New Germany, saluted. "Herr General!"

John Rourke, uncomfortable with the rank imposed upon him by the president of Mid-Wake, didn't know what to do for a moment. To salute in return, he thought, would be silly. He wore no uniform and considered his rank an honorary title more than anything else. Colonel Mann held the salute. John Rourke at last nodded, saying, "Thank you, Colonel," and Mann lowered the salute.

A little girl with long blond ringlets and a very serious expression in her pretty blue eyes was shoved forward out of the crowd of dignitaries. She was so tiny that John Rourke hadn't even noticed her until that instant. She wore a frilly white dress, like something for a formal birthday party. And, in her hands she held flowers. She presented them to him, more or less forcing them toward his hands as he crouched down to her.

"And thank you, too," John Rourke smiled. . . .

An attractive young female officer, an aide to Colonel Mann, announced that the J7-V carrying Sarah, Natalia, Annie, Maria Leuden, and Bjorn Rolvaag had just landed safely. Then the aide retired from the room and Dieter Bern, his fragile-looking frame bent over the table at the center of which were placed the Soviet energy weapons — the one obtained by Jason Darkwood from Mid-Wake, the second secured by Rourke, Paul, and Michael — said, "What a frightening object. Is it not, *mein herren?*"

Paul said, "But how much more frightening in the hands of the enemy alone."

John Rourke looked at his friend, nodding in agreement. "Sir, do your scientists think that the weapon can be duplicated in time to be of some use?"

Dieter Bern's eyebrows shrugged as he looked up.

The room was a formal meeting hall left over from the days of Nazi rule here, overlarge for their purposes, elaborate in the extreme. Black marble quarried in the mountains, Rourke had been told once, comprised the floor and the ceiling, gray marble with yellow gold molding adorning the walls, an immense crystal chandelier suspended on chains from the ceiling directly over the, by comparison, simple dark-stained wooden table around which they were clustered.

Dieter Bern, his voice reedy-sounding from age, at last answered verbally. "Much to my personal regret, but out of necessity, our scientists labor long into each night in the design of weapons. As you no doubt are aware or at least suspect, Herr Doctor, we have even developed thermonuclear warheads and are near completion in the development of long-range delivery systems. At the present, our weapons are crude by comparison to those that your generation used five centuries ago to nearly eradicate all life on earth. But, if the Soviets launch against us, we will at least be able to respond."

" 'Mutually Assured Destruction' is the term, sir," John Rourke responded. "Many persons at that time saw considerable meaning in the English acronym the first letters of those three words form."

"Mad," Wolfgang Mann said solemnly.

Rourke nodded, staring at the energy weapons. "If this device can be perfected in time for use by your troops and the forces of Mid-Wake, these energy weapons may give us the tactical and strategic advantage necessary to prevent that first launch. As we all know, as doubtless your scientists know, even the most modest nuclear exchange could so violently upset our currently quite fragile atmospheric envelope that all life on the surface would perish once again, and the planet would never heal itself. Would life beneath the surface forever be life at all?"

Dieter Bern splayed his long, age-gnarled fingers along the table. "Already, my friend, some of our scientists are laying the foundation necessary to support research into planetary reengineering, much the same as was discussed in the context of the planet Mars before warfare between the super powers so radically changed the course of human history.

"The principles would be, more or less, the same," Bern concluded, "only quite a bit simpler to bring about."

John Rourke lit the cigar he'd placed in his mouth upon first entering the room. He turned the battered Zippo windlighter over in his hands as he exhaled, then looked first at Dieter Bern, then at Wolfgang Mann. "We're talking perhaps as long as a century to accomplish something such as that, at least in the light of your present technology. And planetary engineering, from what little reading I did in the field five centuries ago, worked marvelously well in computer models. But none of those models, even if they were available to you, would be accurate because of the obvious differences in the two planetary bodies. Plus, there'd be the radiation factor to consider . . . how those portions of this planet currently uninhabitable and other portions which might be made so in a new nuclear exchange would bear on the desired results. In the final analysis," Rourke told them, "it's a tremendous gamble. Granted, it may prove necessary, but that possible option having to be exercised should be avoided at all costs."

The table was an elongated rectangle, and Michael had stood silently at the far end for some time. He walked around the table now to be nearer to the devices as he spoke. "If your scientists could push this device to its logical limits, a weapon that could be hand carried and fired and powered by a backpack unit of some type, we could utilize the weapon as a means of obtaining not just battlefield parity, but also a true advantage. What would happen, for example, if my father and Paul and myself, along with your top people and the top people from Mid-Wake, were to penetrate the Soviet Underground City . . . take it and hold it?

"The Soviet forces would be cut off from supply," Michael said, answering his own question. "And, with more of these weapons in the field in German hands and in the hands of the Allied Commando Force that's been formed, we might be able to neutralize the Soviet conventional threat. If we launched a similar attack on the Soviet underwater complex, we might have a chance at effectively interdicting their use of submarine-launched missiles."

Paul spoke. "One thing that was an inescapable reality of the Cold War, Michael, and is a reality now: The primary mission of submarine warfare changed in the period following World War II, when submarines had been utilized only to attack and disrupt shipping and surface maneuvers. Any such roles after the advent of submarine-launched intercontinental ballistic missiles became secondary to the primary mission of attacking land-based targets."

"You see," John Rourke picked up, "the mission of the submarine during the Cold War and in our present situation is to stay hidden. Its conventional weapons array is primarily for the defensive context, so it will uninhibitedly be able to maintain its primary mission goal of being in position to launch its missile battery against land-based targets. Its very mobility is the threat . . . that it can't be neutralized before launch. During the Cold War, sophisticated satellites and other monitoring devices were utilized on both sides to track enemy submarines and plot their positions for interdiction in the event of conflict. Although doubtlessly there's still quite a bit of satellite material still in orbit, even if it were functional, there'd be no way in which to utilize it for tracking. German aircraft haven't the ability to cover the entire Pacific, let along all the world's oceans, in search of enemy submarines. If the Soviets elect to launch a thermonuclear conflict predicated on the invulnerability of their submarine fleet, regardless of the morality concerning the effect on the planet, the logic from a military standpoint is impeccable.

"Mid-Wake," Rourke went on, "has historically fielded a smaller fleet, and its submarines have no such nuclear delivery capability. Our only prayer in the event the Soviets elected to utilize SLICBMs against us would be the Mid-Wake fleet taking out the Soviet fleet. The chances for effectively accomplishing this task without one missile or an entire missile battery being launched would be so low as to be incalculable."

"Are you saying, then, Dr. Rourke—John—that we have lost before the war has begun?" Wolfgang Mann asked, his voice strange-sounding.

"No," John Rourke told Mann, Dieter Bern, and the other Germans. "I'm saying—we're all saying—that we need to strike before they can strike. And, even at that, our chances for success are very slim. That's the reality of the

57

situation. The Soviet presence near Mid-Wake in the Pacific has become the wild card, gentlemen. If the Soviets of the Underground City can manipulate things so there is a coordinated offensive incorporating land forces and the Soviet submarine fleet, we're in very deep trouble."

Chapter Eleven

This had to be the crucial meeting, because it was being held in the official hall of the triumvirate — three very tired-looking old men — the rulers of this Soviet civilization beneath the surface of the Pacific Ocean.

Nicolai Antonovitch sat at the conference table, his eyes drifting over the gray-black marble walls and toward the long desk that dominated the far end of the vaulted chamber. Pillars — of marble or whatever the substance was — supported the roof structure. The desk was empty now, nor did anyone sit behind it. When he had first come here days ago, and after days of negotiation there on the surface, first on the platform, then inside one of the monstrously sized Soviet submarines, he had seen the three men.

They reminded him of Party officials from five centuries ago, the men who had worked behind the scenes and behind the backs of the leaders who had realized the absurdity of global war. And they reminded him of the leader of the Soviet Underground City.

Possessed by their own ability to wield power, they were its prisoners.

Here, Soviet society had crumbled to almost a Stalinist military dictatorship. And the citizens had been relegated to the status of workers within a colony of ants or bees.

No one here besides him had ever seen an ant or bee, because no one here remembered the old days . . . had endured cryogenic sleep carrying him from the horror of the present to new horrors in the future.

He had once been a loyal Communist and in his heart still believed in Communism. It was the men who practiced it, who ruled through it, who were the ones that corrupted it. But, did not mankind corrupt all that it touched?

And Antonovitch suddenly wondered what he was doing here.

He had come for the sole purpose of effecting an alliance that would bring about the destruction of mankind. He knew that, just as surely as he knew that if he did not do this thing, the next man behind him would forge the alliance in his stead.

And the woman, Dr. Svetlana Alexsova.

She sat opposite him, chatting gaily with the Soviet military leaders. and each night slept in his bed. But he would not, at least in the figurative sense, turn his back on her. She served the State and herself. He was only her tool.

Behind the desk the wall of marble was smooth, but he knew that set within the wall was a door, all but seamless. And he watched for the three men to emerge from that portion of the wall now.

And then the final round of talks would begin.

They would share the power, thus dividing the Earth that would be the spoils of this war to end all wars forever, because there would be no one left alive to fight another war. The situation would have been humorous in a black comedy sense, a group of vile little boys planning to divide a ball into segments after playing and winning a game that would destroy the ball forever.

But no one understood that as he did.

To them, the chance of destruction was a risk to be taken.

To him, destruction was not a risk; it was a certainty.

Chapter Twelve

There was to be a formal dinner tonight, Natalia was told shortly after their arrival. The people of New Germany in Argentina did not utilize money, but rather—like something out of the science fiction novels so popular in the twentieth century—a system of credits, hence credit cards. Such a credit card was presented to her, and identical ones—save for the names and registration numbers—were given to Sarah, Annie, and Maria.

Sarah and Maria had gone off together, and Natalia was now alone with Annie—alone save for the seemingly thousands of other persons milling about the streets and byways of the German city.

And to Natalia, after all this time, any sort of crowd was difficult to adjust to.

She wore the only "decent" clothes she'd brought with her, having thought more along the lines of fighting than shopping, and for once saw some advantages to Annie's more normally formal attire. Except when situations demanded otherwise, even in the field, Annie wore a skirt. As they walked down the street a friendly policewoman had directed them toward, Natalia looked at Annie and smiled. "Isn't this absurd?"

"Shopping? You used to be able to shop. I've never been able to shop. What do you do?"

"Well, you walk around the store and pretend as if you're disinterested, but always politely disinterested. A salesperson comes up to you and asks if you need help. You tell her you're just looking, and she tells you to call if you need any assistance. You keep walking around and then the saleswoman comes up to you again, asks what you're looking for. You tell her in general terms, and she immediately shows you something she thinks would look perfect for your purposes. Then you tell her you're still just looking around, and you eventually find something you want to try on. Well, then you find the saleswoman and she shows you where to change, and when you come out, wearing it, she tells you it looks lovely on you."

"What if it doesn't?"

"That's why they have mirrors," Natalia laughed.

Michael Rourke considered his options as he cleaned his pistols. All of his options, of course, were predicated on survival of the coming battles for the domination of the Earth. But, if his side was victorious, then what?

He was a grown man of thirty years old, and he had no truly marketable skills other than those related to warfare. He had, ever since his father had awakened them, spent five years with them and then returned to The Sleep, telling himself that, someday, he would be a doctor . . . a doctor like his father.

Michael Rourke wondered now if that would ever happen.

And New Germany made his concerns all the more real. Because here, in New Germany, was probably the finest medical school on the present-day Earth. Even without competition, it was more advanced by far than anything that had existed in the days his father had attended school.

And here, in New Germany, Maria Leuden was in her familiar surroundings, where she belonged.

He loved her, but did he belong here? Could he belong anywhere?

And did he love her enough?

For the thousandth or millionth or billionth time, Michael Rourke opened his wallet and studied one photograph there . . . Madison, beautiful in her wedding dress, standing beside him.

He had always thought she looked like the popular concept of an angel, and now she was among them, apart from him forever; or, if there was a Heaven and by some fluke, with all the death and destruction to his credit, he was admitted there, apart from her until his death.

In an odd way—a way in which he somehow felt ashamed for even considering—he was somewhat comforted that she was not alone. Their unborn child had gone to death and to the grave with her.

He'd sometimes pictured himself if, somehow, Madison had died after the birth of their child. What would he have told his son or daughter about its mother?

He would have told the child, he knew, that she had been incredibly lovely, incredibly gentle, incredibly loving, and that she had returned to the place of her origin, with the angels, where she waited, watching over them.

Tears filled Michael Rourke's eyes, and he sat down on the edge of the bed in his room and whispered her name. But "Madison" didn't sound quite right, because his throat was so tight, so choked.

Chapter Thirteen

The two women pausing before the shop window looked more or less like all the other women on the streets of the city, except perhaps that they were prettier than most. One of them — the tall one with the almost black, just-past-shoulder-length hair, wearing a white blouse and nearly ankle-length khaki skirt, and carrying an enormous black cloth shoulder bag — was exquisite. She was Major Natalia Anastasia Tiemerovna, Committee for State Security of the Soviet. The other one had dark honey-colored hair that was much longer, cascading to her trim waist. She reminded him of photos he'd seen in history books of the decadent twentieth-century hippies of postwar Germany and America. Her dress, as long as the major's skirt, was an explosion of autumnal colors. And peeking out from beneath its hem were boots. A long, wide scarf was draped over one of her shoulders, in a red so deep it was almost the color of blood. She carried a purse but somehow looked awkward with it. Otherwise, she was as beautiful as the darker-haired major, just more little girl-like, less sophisticated-seeming.

Perhaps there was, in fact, a means of accounting for this Annie person's marriage to the Jew, Rubenstein. Did the blood of an equally inferior race flow through her veins . . . that of gypsies? He had thought gypsies extinct, but supposedly they had such wild looks and wild ways about them. The Annie person was laughing.

He nodded to Carl, who watched from the other side of the street. Carl removed his hat, ran his fingers back through his thinning hair — the signal — and moved off.

He watched the two women for a moment longer. With the shoulder bags they carried, they might well be armed.

That would make no difference. Carl was not a pleasant fellow, but he was very efficient at killing. It was Carl who had assassinated the wife of the traitorous Wolfgang Mann, not far from here really, killing two of the traitorous Dieter Bern's soldiers in the course of his escape.

Carl, indeed, had a knack for his work . . . enjoyed it.

The two women had moved on and now paused before another shop window, talking, both laughing, it seemed. And then the one who fornicated with the Jew, Rubenstein, did something with her clothes, turning around a full three hundred sixty degrees. Then both women laughed again. They hugged each other briefly as they laughed. Lesbians? That thought amused him.

Then the two women went inside the shop.

He watched the shop for a moment longer, then walked away. . . .

"Ohh, I like this—for you, I mean," Annie enthused. She looked at Natalia's pretty blue eyes, her face. But Natalia was looking at the dress rather oddly. "Don't you like it?"

"Annie, I just don't think it's me, that's all."

"You'd look sensational in green."

"The beadwork . . . I mean, I just don't think so."

Annie nodded. "You want to look more like a princess than a party girl," Annie said. "Fine. We'll both look like princesses." And she took an off-white formal from the rack, swept it in front of her dramatically, and threw her left arm up and back. "Ohh, my dear, aren't we just too divine!"

Natalia laughed, saying, "Be serious a little or we'll never find anything in time to wear tonight."

"Right," Annie told her, suppressing a giggle. Her eyes caught a movement just beyond the window there on the walkway. Why was a man staring so intently into a dress shop? He walked on.

"What's wrong?"

"Some guy outside, that's all."

Natalia turned around and glanced toward the windows. "I don't see him."

"Never mind," Annie told her. "Ohh, look at this!" She took another dress from the rack of formals. It was blue, very plain, very elegant. "Talk about princesses," she said.

So far, Natalia had spotted five men, and she was tempted to go to the first German policeman or soldier and report it. But if there were to be an attack and it would be unfocused because it occurred off schedule, many innocent lives might be lost.

Just because someone — a soldier or a police officer — carried a firearm, there was no reason to suppose that person would be wonderfully proficient in its use. She and Annie could have left the shopping area, gotten themselves out of harm's way. But postponing the inevitable was nothing she'd ever relished, and if an attack were aimed at them, a similar attack might be aimed at Sarah and Maria.

So, the thing to do was force the situation.

For that, she needed to make both Annie and herself appear as irresistibly vulnerable as possible — and very quickly.

The store was called "Olga's," and had, by far, the finest selection of any they had visited.

There was a beautiful white dress, but Natalia had no tan and the color would only have made her appear paler than she usually looked. She found the perfect thing in black, and despite her height, it seemed as though with a few quick alterations it would be ideal.

Annie had found a dress as well, also in black. "Ohh, we shouldn't—"

"It will be fun, wearing the same color. Let's try them on," Natalia volunteered. There were closetlike booths at the rear of the store, with doors similar to those used in restrooms, the doors starting about eighteen inches off the floor so the legs of the person behind them were visible.

66

The entire booth was constructed similarly, freestanding in a block side-by-side, each sharing a common wall with the next. They were positioned just a short distance from a rear wall of the shop, behind which probably lay some sort of storage area. The idea that had come to Natalia when they'd first entered the store was now something she was certain of.

They started toward the changing area, Natalia whispering under her breath, "There are five of them, I think, and they'll try to kill us while we're changing. You're wearing boots, so you'll have to be the maneuver element." They stopped beside a table and examined junk jewelry. "When we get into the booths, we'll be side-by-side. If we can't get two next to one another, we'll find something else to look at and wait. When we get inside we talk, just loud enough so that anyone listening will know we're inside. You get out of your boots and leave them standing in the exact center of the space, so anyone looking from the front will see them . . . think you're in them. I'll keep talking to you after you've left and let my skirt drop to the floor."

"Where am I going?"

"Crawl out under the back wall of the booth, lose yourself in the racks, and get a position of concealment from which you can observe the entrance and the booths. When the men rush in, open up on them and I'll open fire from the booth. We'll have them in a crossfire, neat and clean."

"You could get killed."

"Don't worry; then I wouldn't get to wear this dress."

"All right," Annie agreed.

There were two booths side-by-side. Natalia and Annie walked toward them, entering them but not too quickly. Natalia closed the door behind her. "Annie?" Natalia said in a voice just loud enough to be noticeable.

"Yes?"

"Do you still have those black pearls?" Annie didn't have any black pearls.

"And I brought them with me, too!"

67

"Ohh, good! They'd look wonderful with your dress or mine." Natalia looked toward the floor. Stocking-footed, Annie was crawling out under the back partition. Natalia kicked out of her shoes. "You know, it was really good luck coming in here, Annie." She had the suppressor fitted stainless steel PPK/S American out of her purse, hanging it by the trigger guard on a hook on the partition nearest her right hand. She unbuttoned the waistband of her skirt, thumbed it down over her hips, and shrugged the garment to the floor around her ankles. She reached into the neckline of her blouse and tucked the solitary spare magazine she had for the PPK/S into the cleavage between her breasts. "I wish we'd known about this banquet tonight. I don't even have any good shoes. We're going to have to find some, Annie. What?" She paused for an instant, as if listening to Annie. "That's a good idea!" She had one of the two evening gowns in her left hand (the one she wasn't planning on buying, just in case it took a stray bullet) and her pistol in her right hand, the little .380's slide mounted thumb safety up and off. "Ohh, all right, you can use it, but I thought you didn't like that scent." She hoped, if the men were already in the store and listening, her conversation sounded vacuous enough. She peered through the crack between the door and the side wall, and she thought she saw men's shoes near a rack of hostess skirts.

And then Annie, from about twenty feet away, to the right and nearer the front of the store, shouted so loudly she could have awakened the dead, "Now, Natalia!"

Natalia kicked the stall door open and threw herself left and down, going into a roll as the first shots came. Annie's .45 boomed earsplitting in the confines of the shop, the chatter of an M16 starting as Natalia came up on her knees. Four men were clearly visible, a fifth on the floor already dead. Natalia's right hand raised instinctively as she pulled the Walther's trigger through double action and shot the man with the chopped-down M16 through the right temple.

68

She swung the muzzle of the PPK/S, Annie's .45 and Natalia's .380 discharging almost simultanously, killing a third man holding a Beretta 92F in both hands as he was just turning to fire on her. The last two men broke for the doors.

Annie fired, then fired again, one of the men pitching forward through the window glass and onto the sidewalk. But he picked himself up, stumbling into a run at the heels of the other man.

Natalia was already running after him, jumping over one of the dead men, careful of her stockinged feet as she ran past the broken glass into the pedestrian walkway. The few private vehicles were already knotting into what would pass for a traffic jam here, and jaws dropped as faces turned toward her . . . a woman in a blouse with only the bottom part of a silk teddy covering the lower portion of her body, a gun in her hand; Natalia, never considering herself an exhibitionist, laughed at the thought. The wounded man tripped and fell, pushing a pistol toward her as a female pedestrian near him screamed.

Natalia moved into a crouch and held the Walther in both hands as she fired. The sound of the suppressor-fitted pistol's report was best compared, she'd always thought, to the sound she'd first heard five centuries ago while posing as an American housewife on an assignment for the KGB. It sounded identical—to her, at least—to the loud plop made when one cracked open a tubular package of oven-ready biscuits against a countertop.

She fired again, then again, hitting the man in the throat and the left eyeball, all three shots killing ones.

The last man turned toward her and fired. Natalia dropped to the pavement, running her nylons as at least two shots sang past her. Annie screamed from behind her, "Watch out! He's got a hostage!"

Natalia was changing magazines for the PPK/S as she rolled over the curb and into the street, coming up on both knees, the pistol at maximum extension of both arms.

"Don't!" Natalia shouted to the fifth man.

The last of the assassins sent against her and Annie, thinning hair visible under what these days passed for a man's fedora, held the muzzle of a Beretta 92F to the head of a woman about Natalia's own age, the woman very obviously pregnant and very obviously terrified.

Police and soldiers were filling the street, orders barked in strident German, the assassin unwavering as he held the woman before him as a shield. Annie, stocking-footed, was walking forward slowly, her ScoreMaster .45 held in a point shoulder position.

A German officer shouted to Natalia, ordering her to drop her weapon. Natalia shouted back to him in his own language. "I am Natalia Tiemerovna! Do not interfere here or your Colonel Mann will hear of it! Dispatch personnel to locate Sarah Rourke and her party; there may be a similar assassination team ready to assault them. Do it now!"

And she proceeded to ignore his further protestations as, slowly, she got up from her knees, the muzzle of the Walther still aimed at the assassin's head. "Damned hat," she murmured under her breath. Without the hat, she could have gotten a clear enough idea of the actual size of his head so she could shoot him there. "Annie! Come up slowly and keep to your side."

"Right."

The assassin, in surprisingly good English, shouted to her, "If you attempt to—"

"To do what?" Natalia screamed back at him. "You'll kill her? Then you'll die! If you don't lay down that pistol now, then you will die. If you do lay it down, I promise you your life—if you cooperate." She was trying to read what kind of man this was. Was he insane enough to kill the pregnant woman hostage and go down in a hail of bullets? Or was there enough rationality left to him that he would take this one chance? If she could keep him talking, even just a little longer, there was always the chance he might surrender, but a better chance still that she could make a killing shot.

The Beretta he held . . . how had they gotten these American military weapons that had been stored for the returning Eden Project? The Beretta was cocked, his right first finger inside the guard and resting against the trigger. A shot to the elbow would have the best chance of success against an involuntary reflex triggering the shot to the head of the hostage.

"I will kill her, Fräulein Major!"

"Then I will kill you. You are not dealing with police, the military, anyone in this but Annie and me. We don't negotiate, listen to demands. You will surrender or you will die here, Nazi!"

"Don't come any closer!"

Natalia felt that she was close enough. "Let her go and you live; my word as an officer!"

There was indecision in his eyes.

But Natalia had decided. "Annie!"

As Natalia called Annie's name, to momentarily distract the assassin — she hoped — she triggered the shot from the Walther, the bullet striking the underside of the man's elbow, the Beretta flying from his grasp as the pregnant woman screamed. The assassin fell back, his left hand sweeping up from under his jacket.

Natalia had wanted him alive. There was no choice now, her body already moving, her right first finger already squeezing back against the trigger. The PPK/S discharged, Annie's .45 firing a microsecond after it. The assassin's left hand held a second Beretta. He triggered a shot into the sidewalk in the same instant that his body rocked back, a bullet hole where his right eyeball had been and a second wound in his throat just under his chin. Natalia's second bullet hit her original target, the man's right temple.

And then the police and the military were all over him, the pregnant woman pulled away as though she were still in danger.

Natalia looked to the left, then the right. Annie was stepping back. Natalia interposed her thumb between the

Walther's hammer and the rear face of the slide and worked the safety to drop the hammer, rolling her thumb out as it fell.

She exhaled.

Chapter Fourteen

The meeting had already dragged on interminably, it seemed. Antonovitch waited for a break between sentences and interrupted the principal of the three triumvirate members. "Comrades, it would seem to me, if I might interject, that a very simple situation confronts us."

All three of the triumvirate members looked at him. Across the table from him, Dr. Alexsova smiled, the smile pretty, her eyes boring into him.

Antonovitch pressed on before one of the other two triumvirate members began another long monologue or the leader resumed the one that Antonovitch had just interrupted. "We are all Communists, we are all Russians, so why do we waste valuable time and energies in this debate? Already, I have been given to understand, several vessels of your submarine fleet have crossed through the Drake Passage and have stationed themselves in the South Atlantic off the Argentine coast."

The naval officer sitting beside Svetlana Alexsova interrupted, saying, "The area which you refer to as the Drake Passage, Comrade General, is known as the Stalin Passage."

Antonovitch smiled. Hard-line Communists, the same as he dealt with at the Underground City. They had to be, to memorialize a dictator like Joseph Stalin. "As you say, Comrade Admiral, the Stalin Passage. But, with your vessels in position for attack on New Germany, would not all of our interests be better served by planning what should transpire rather than debating future global politics?"

The head of the triumvirate, as dour-faced and grey a man as Antonovitch had ever seen, answered, "Comrade General Antonovitch, we are aware of the military urgency to which you alude. But we are not mercenaries, fighting for a cause because of some Capitalistic profit motives, nor do we send our gallant young Communists into battle merely in answer to a request. No. There must be covenants between our Communist brothers on the land and ourselves, because without such agreements, our fleet will not fire, will not support your land forces. And, without our thermonuclear weapons, Comrade, the people of your Underground City cannot triumph . . . will go down in defeat."

Antonovitch lit a cigarette, partially because he wanted one, partially because he knew that smoking irritated the head of the triumvirate. "Comrades, must I remind you that if we, your brothers—as you have so generously referred to us—should be defeated, then the combined forces which will have engineered that defeat will be able to turn their free attentions to you, in aid of their ally Mid-Wake. And then what? With backs to the wall, you will utilize your nuclear warheads, and if the evidence our scientists and the scientists of our enemies have amassed proves true, you make the Earth forever uninhabitable. Not just the surface atmosphere will disappear, but the oceans themselves will vaporize this time. How long would your underwater complex last here? A few seconds? No. The only way in which there can be a Communist victory without bringing about the destruction of humanity as a species, Comrades, is by combining our forces now, utilizing your submarine fleet as the launching platforms for missiles carrying conventional warheads, to devastate our enemies and bring them to their knees. Otherwise, we are all dead, all of us on both sides."

Antonovitch did not like the way in which Svetlana Alexsova just looked at him.

Chapter Fifteen

By the time John Rourke heard what had happened, he also had full information concerning the results of the assassination attempt. There had been no team dispatched after Sarah and Maria, and the killers sent to murder Natalia and his daughter Annie had themselves been killed.

He dressed for the ridiculous dinner party being held in his honor, better things to do than this. "Temper," Rourke told himself. Even though he was, technically, a general, he had no uniform—nor would he have worn one if he had. Hence, he fell back to the uniform of formal dinner parties for nearly six centuries now, the tuxedo.

In the five centuries since he had last worn one, nothing had changed. Five centuries ago, lapels had swung pendulum fashion from wide to narrow, to wide to narrow again, then back to wide, and shirt collars had gone from the wing type—which he personally detested—to more standard collars, then back to the wing type again.

Two tailors from New Germany's most exclusive men's clothiers had arrived at the unneccssarily large apartment he had been given for his use, bringing with them a large variety of formal clothes. After realizing it was puerile to protest, Rourke submitted to the inevitable, but selected from among the clothes the most conservative, those closest to the solitary tuxedo he had owned Before the Night of the War.

Black.

The lapels were of a medium width.

He eschewed a cummerbund just as vigorously now as he had then.

The shirts—why did they insist he needed a half dozen?—were plain-fronted, requiring studs, and had the standard type of collar featured on those designed for less splendiferous purposes.

The ties—three—were neither ultrasmall nor the size of a mutated butterfly, but essentially identical to the tie—one—he had used five centuries ago. He had, of course, opted now, as then, for the sort of tie one did oneself.

And, just as it had been five centuries ago, a tuxedo was damnably difficult for hiding any sort of substantial handgun. A curious coincidence, he thought, reflecting on it now as he knotted his tie. But when he and Paul and Michael had stopped at The Retreat to pick up Sarah, Natalia, Annie, and Maria, during the course of a fast inspection of The Retreat systems, he'd checked the gun cabinets, of course, not just the glass case that was in the open in the Great Room, but the other storage areas as well. He'd stored the CAR-15 he no longer had the luxury of carrying in its proper place, returning the Colt Lawman two-incher as well, since he no longer carried a companion .357 Magnum revolver, his Metalifed and Mag-Na-Ported Python having been damaged beyond easy repair some time ago. But he'd noticed a handgun he thought might prove useful, one of the last guns he'd acquired Before the Night of the War.

He'd bought it for practical as well as for emotional reasons back then. When he would occasionally confer with an influential friend at Smith & Wesson, he would ask the same questions that apparently many thousands of other Smith & Wesson fans had on their minds: "Any plans to produce the old Centennial Model in stainless steel?"

When the gun eventually was produced that way, sans grip safety and in the more rust-resistant form, Rourke held out for some time, telling himself there were better things he could spend his money on than another firearm. But, in the end, he'd acquired it. The telling thing was the Centennials were tested for Plus P Plus, so he could safely fire ordinary Plus P .38 Special through the gun.

Although the handgun came with nicely figured smooth Goncalo Alves stocks, he immediately removed these and substituted, instead, a Barami Hip Grip. The Hip Grip, on those rare occasions when he would carry a short-barrelled

J- or K-Frame revolver, had always proved itself as the most concealable way.

Before he closed up the case in which he'd found the Model 640 Centennial, he decided to take it along.

A modest supply of new manufacture .38 Special made for him by the Germans but to the exact specifications of the old Federal 158-grain Semi-Wadcutted Lead Hollowpoint Plus P loading, a spare set of the Hip Grips, a solitary Safariland J-Frame speedloader, and he was set, stashing the gun in his pack for some future use as an emergency hide-out.

The bow tie knotted, John Rourke went to the pack that lay on the foot of one of the two double beds. Sarah would return to their room in a few moments, but he had a meeting to attend before the banquet, so time was of the essence.

He extracted the Centennial from the pack, checked it for functional reliability, loaded it with five of the SWLHPs, then slipped the revolver on its Hip Grip into the beltless waistband of his trousers, taking the A.G. Russell Sting IA Black Chrome from the dresser top where his other weapons lay and securing knife and sheath near the small of his back.

As Rourke was about to slip into his jacket, the door to the apartment opened and he left the bedroom. It was Sarah.

She wasn't ready yet, of course, but looked lovely nonetheless. Her hair, not quite as long as Annie's, was softly arranged, drawn back at the nape of her neck. She was dressed simply, as was her habit, in a pretty pastel floral print maternity-style top—something Annie had made for her, he surmised—a blue skirt, and low-heeled shoes.

"Hi."

"Hi," Rourke smiled.

"Annie and Natalia . . . that was terrible. Annie told me all about it. Thank God they were together."

"Yes. You look very pretty."

She smiled at him. "You look pretty." John Rourke didn't know what to say and he cleared his throat. "So, I'll see you at dinner?"

"Yes."

She started to walk toward the bedroom, Rourke deferring to her as she went through the doorway, following her. She stopped before the dresser. "You're leaving your Detonics .45's?"

"Won't carry under a tuxedo unless it's tailored for them or the jacket's a couple of sizes too large, at least in the shoulder holsters."

She turned around and looked at him as he slipped into his coat, coming closer to him and putting the palms of her hands against his chest. "What are we going to do? I mean, if we lose this big battle everyone's starting to talk about, we don't have to worry about it. But, if we win—"

"I love you and I always have loved you."

"And you love Natalia, too, John. I know that, and in a way I've come to accept that."

John Rourke folded Sarah into his arms. He touched his lips to her forehead. "You're my wife."

"The consolation prize?"

"I never said that," he told her, still holding her.

"You know what's the interesting thing, John? I can really understand why you love her. She's extraordinary, not just the way she looks or what she can do, but she's extraordinary."

"So are you."

She leaned up and kissed him lightly on the mouth. "Big deal what I can do, John. Or anything else about me. But she's so much like you, and maybe she's just a little bit better, and maybe that's what's so intriguing about her."

"Uhh . . ." He didn't know what to say, which was always his problem, he realized.

"You gave me two fine children." Then Sarah touched her abdomen gently. "Three. At least Dr. Munchen told me he doesn't think we'll have twins, and I didn't want an ultrasound or any of the newer tests. And you love me. It's all right that you love Natalia, John. It wasn't your fault. And whatever you decide, I know it'll be the right thing for all of us."

78

John Rourke held her more tightly and kissed her hair, remembering why he'd first told her he loved her more than five centuries ago.

Some things did not change.

Chapter Sixteen

A lit cigar in his clenched teeth, John Rourke entered the meeting hall they had used earlier.

A half-dozen German Long Range Mountain Patrol guards under the command of a senior sergeant stood guard at the doors. Rourke was admitted without question.

Seated in a chair, wearing his dress uniform, was Jason Darkwood. Standing beside him, arm still in a sling, was Sam Aldridge in Marine Corps Dress Blues. Otto Hammerschmidt stood by the window, deep in discussion, it seemed, with Colonel Mann, both German officers in dress uniform.

Neither Michael nor Paul had arrived yet.

Nor had Dieter Bern.

Rourke crossed to Jason Darkwood in three long strides, Darkwood starting to stand. "Relax, Captain. How are you feeling?"

"Full of antibiotics and bandaged in a few uncomfortable places and a little tired. But okay."

"I know the feeling," Rourke smiled, starting to offer his right hand to shake, but remembering he'd just removed the bandages from both his hands less than an hour ago. "Forgive me," and he nodded toward his hands. "Still a little tender."

"You're out of uniform, General."

"Yeah, right," Rourke smiled good-naturedly. "And that's the way I intend to stay. Remember?" Rourke joked. "A general has a right to make his own uniform, which means I'm not out of uniform at all, am I?"

"Touché."

Sam Aldridge laughed sonorously.

The doors to the chamber opened again, and Michael and Paul entered, Rourke staring at them. He'd never before seen either man in a tuxedo, and seeing his son dressed that way was an experience he doubted he'd ever forget. He thought, My God, he's grown up!"

"Dad, Dr. Bern will be along in a little while. One of his aides met us in the corridor."

"Thanks, son," Rourke nodded. Now he studied their attire more clinically. Where were Michael's Beretta 92Fs? Where was Paul's Browning High Power? Mentally, he gave them each high marks, knowing neither of them would have traveled unarmed any more than he would. He looked away, not wanting to find the spots where they'd hidden their guns. "Well, gentlemen, a party coming up. How nice, and how useless."

From the windows where he still stood, Wolfgang Mann called out, "Yes, but the habiliments of civilization are important at times, aren't they, Doctor?"

Rourke looked over his shoulder toward Mann and smiled. "I suppose. But I'll confess I'd enjoy the prospects of this banquet more if it were for some purpose other than what I understand it to be."

"You will be awarded the Knight's Cross, Herr Doctor. Few men have earned such a distinction."

Rourke had not realized he was to be given a medal. "Look, I don't—"

"You didn't know!" Mann exclaimed, leaving the company of Otto Hammerschmidt suddenly and crossing the room toward Rourke. "Forgive me, Herr Doctor!"

"Forgiven, but I really don't—"

"I knew," Paul said, "and so did Michael. I mean, John, without you, who of us would be here? The German Republic would still be a Nazi dictatorship, and . . . well, if anyone deserves a medal, you do."

John Rourke looked at his friend, then down at his hand, realizing he needed to find an ashtray but couldn't, instead tapping ashes into his left palm as he cupped it. "All I ever did—"

But before Rourke could complete his thought, the doors opened again and Dieter Bern entered, positively withered-looking in an ill-fitting, impossibly overlarge tuxedo that, like its wearer, appeared to have seen better days. "Gentlemen, it appears from our latest reconnaissance overflights that the Russians have stationed several of their undersea boats off our coastline."

John Rourke looked at Colonel Mann. "And this is the time for a party?"

But Deiter Bern continued to speak. "If they intend the use of nuclear missiles, we are all dead. If not, it is their move in any event. I suggest that we utilize the evening to its fullest potential, gentlemen. Tonight we live, while tomorrow we might die."

John Thomas Rourke looked at his son and his friend, then at his son again. What sort of life had Michael lived until now? A dead wife and baby? A mistress. Was that all?

And he looked at his friend, his son-in-law. What had Paul and Annie had?

As he flicked more ashes into his palm, John Rourke answered his own question.

They had lived all that life allowed them.

It was time he did the same.

Chapter Seventeen

Natalia entered the ballroom and the music should have stopped.

John Rourke's heart nearly did.

She walked at Paul's right, Annie, beautiful as well, at his left. Both women wore black.

A short distance behind them walked Michael, his mother at his left arm, his mistress, Maria Leuden, as his right. Sarah's pregnancy was barely detectable with the dark blue floor-length gown she wore, and Marie Leuden, her glasses absent, her hair up, wore a floor-length, bare-shouldered dress of pale green.

The military orchestra played a waltz-tempoed German pop song Rourke did not recognize beyond origin, but it was pretty enough and he walked across the ballroom floor, threading his way past the dancing couples, straight toward Sarah.

She looked up at him. "Dance with me?" Rourke asked his wife.

She came into his arms as he drew her out onto the floor.

"You're beautiful," he told her honestly.

She leaned her head against his chest for a moment.

"I understand we're supposed to drink and dance and have a good time for a while yet until the banquet, then more drinking and dancing and having a good time."

"You're getting a medal, John."

"Yes," Rourke drawled out, his eyes surveying the floor without even consciously trying. "That young officer who's Hammerschmidt's brother . . . he deserves a medal. Darkwood deserves a medal."

"I hear he'll get once once he returns to Mid-Wake. And he's getting one here tonight."

Rourke looked down into his wife's gray-green eyes. "Anything else happening this evening I don't know about?"

"It depends. What do you have in mind?"

Rourke smiled, drawing her closer against him. . . .

"I am empowered," Antonovitch said wearily, "to offer half of all territories to be conquered and our full logistical support technologically and otherwise in your reclamation efforts associated with these lands. All of this in exchange for your full cooperation in prosecution of the war effort against the Allies and your turning over to us ten percent of your submarine fleet plus whatever Mid-Wake vessels might be captured, with, of course, your full support for our successful operation of these vessels."

The head of the triumvirate smiled, folding his hands on the conference table. "Ten percent of our fleet? The Mid-Wake vessels are yours, but this ten percent —"

"I can assure you, Comrade, that your forces would be more than compensated. You would have full right to all armored vehicles and surface weapons technology captured from the Allies, as well as ten percent of our armor, to include the mobile missile launchers we discussed earlier."

"And the Particle Beam weapons technology, Comrade General? Would you share this with us?"

"I am not authorized to do so, Comrade. But such details as these would be open to discussion in the future."

"We should, of course, be prepared to share with you our nuclear warheads."

Antonovitch smiled. "But following a victory over the Allies, Comrade, of what use would such devices be to either of us? And, as I have said, if we utilize these missiles during the conflict, we will all suffer the consequences. The nuclear missiles figure into our overall strategic plans as a Sword of Damocles only, to —"

The admiral asked, "A Sword of what?"

Svetlana Alexsova answered for Antonovitch. "In the mythology of an ancient land known as Greece, a sword was suspended over a man's head on a single thread. If the thread broke, the sword would fall and kill him. If it did not, he was spared."

The head of the triumvirate said, "Then under no circumstances would we utilize our nuclear missiles?"

"We would be committing racial suicide, Comrades, were we to do that. But the Germans and Americans at Mid-Wake will believe that we will use them if necessary, therefore holding back."

The admiral asked, "Does not your intelligence suggest that the Germans are perfecting nuclear capabilities?"

"Yes, but—"

"If they are sufficiently far along, not only can these missiles be used against land-based targets, but also against ourselves here beneath the sea. It would not be difficult for the submarine vessel captured by the war criminal Darkwood, which has a full complement of missiles fitted with conventional warheads, to be turned to our destruction merely by utilizing the German warheads."

"It is not my fault, Comrade Admiral, that one of your submarines was stolen, but the likelihood of such a development in time for it to be of any consequence against us is highly remote," Antonovitch asserted, lighting another cigarette. "If we strike now, your vessels will catch the German defenses by surprise. My land forces will attack. We could achieve a major victory. At the very least, we will so severely weaken our adversaries that they will never fully recover. The Allies, without a manufacturing base in New Germany or in Mid-Wake, would be powerless to resupply.

"A full company of Elite Corps Commandoes stand ready to join with your Marine Spetznas' personnel," Antonovitch told them, "in an assault on Mid-Wake. If we can even severely damage both technological centers—New Germany and Mid-Wake—victory is ours."

"And what do you say, Comrade Doctor Alexsova?"

Antonovitch stared at Svetlana Alexsova, then at the triumvirate head. "Why do you ask?"

"I have curiosity for the scientific perspective, Comrade

85

General," the old man smiled.

Svetlana Alexsova folded her hands at the very edge of the table, looked at Antonovitch for a split second over the rims of her glasses, then said, "All which General Antonovitch says is true, Comrade, of course. But the argument that the atmospheric envelope would be irreparably damaged by one or even a few nuclear detonations is theory at best, based on computer models. Indeed—"

"Svetlana!" Antonovitch said, standing up.

"Indeed," she continued, ignoring him, "the Particle Beam technology may be sufficient to defeat the Allied land forces and allow total concentration then on the forces of your historic American enemies at Mid-Wake, but should the energy weapons—which were developed," she added, removing her glasses, smiling, "under my direction—should they prove inadequate to the task, then we must be militarily and psychologically prepared, Comrades, to use the warheads."

Antonovitch stood there, wanting to say something but not knowing what.

She looked up at him. "I speak on full authority of our government."

"What are you—?"

She smiled at him, cocking her eyebrows as she responded. "A realist, Comrade? I did not endure the nuclear war in the era from which you survived. Therefore, perhaps I have a clearer perspective, can view the events unfolding before us with a degree of objectivity greater than yours, Comrade. If the Allied forces on the surface are vaporized, what does it matter so long as Communism triumphs?"

"What does it matter? Are you insane? We would all die because the planet would no longer be capable of supporting human life . . . any life."

"Speculation, only speculation."

Antonovitch sat down heavily in his chair.

The head of the triumverate spoke. "I will order the commander of our fleet stationed off the coast of Argentina to await coordinates from your forces so the missile bombardment of New Germany can begin in coordination with your surface attack."

Antonovitch heard the words but did not look at the man. He looked at Svetlana Alexsova's eyes. He saw madness there.

Chapter Eighteen

White table-clothed round tables accommodating eight persons each were placed about the banquet hall, the head table on a long dais overlooking these, the German officer corps and government functionaries out in such seeming full strength Rourke wondered half seriously who was minding the front. In addition to the Germans and their spouses, there were quite a number of unaccompanied officers from Mid-Wake, some from the First Chinese City, among both officer corps, faces Rourke readily recognized. Bjorn Rolvaag was the only Icelandic.

Rourke and his family sat at the head table, along with Jason Darkwood, Sam Aldridge, Otto Hammerschmidt, and Hammerschmidt's younger brother. Dieter Bern had just concluded speaking — in English, in deference to those non-German speakers in his audience — and now Wolfgang Mann ascended to the podium. "We are here tonight to pay honor to several brave men, two of them American and one of them German.

"But although we specifically honor these three men," he went on, "we honor all men and women tonight who so honor freedom that they willingly risk their lives. We sit here tonight knowing that at any moment our units might be called up in the event of an attack by the Soviet Forces who have penetrated New Germany, and off our shore lie the undersea boats of still a second Soviet power."

There were murmurs throughout the audience now, hurried looks one to another among the officers, both senior and junior. But Colonel Mann continued speaking. "Most symbolic of our fight is one man. His name is Dr. John Thomas Rourke."

Rourke looked down into his drink.

"The good Herr Doctor is, indeed, the rallying point, the focus of our fight. Without his help, those of us who are citizens of New Germany would still be living beneath the heel of a tyrant leader who espoused the vile philosophy of Naziism, suppressing all free thought. Those of us here tonight from the First Chinese City might well have been crushed by the Soviet war machine had it not been for Dr. Rourke's courageous leadership in preventing the Soviets from obtaining the nuclear missiles of the Second Chinese City. Indeed, all of us might have suffered . . . died. And Lydveldid Island. Tonight we are honored by the presence of one of the heroic Icelandics, a humble officer of the law. Lydveldid Island, too, owes its debts to John Rourke.

"And let us not forget Mid-Wake, the last bastion of the United States of America, a city beneath the waters of the Pacific which, for five centuries, has single-handedly and heroically combatted the Soviet Communist war machine. Here, too, John Rourke played an important role.

"John Rourke. Although all assembled here tonight know his name as well as their own, not all of us know very much more about him. I conferred with his heroic wife, Sarah . . . with his son and his daughter and his friends. I will share with you some of what I have learned," Mann said.

Rourke wanted to escape. There was nowhere to run.

"John Thomas Rourke was born during what is often called 'The Cold War,' the only child of an American agent who fought against Germany during World War Two. It appears that fighting Naziism may be something in the Herr Doctor's blood." There was a little laughter, then Mann continued. "John Rourke trained to become a physician, but after completion of medical training he joined the United States Intelligence organization known as the CIA, or Central Intelligence Agency. During those years, he fought against the forces of Communism in our very own South America and elsewhere throughout the globe.

"The Herr Doctor left the CIA to teach and write. Peaceful pursuits, one might indeed say, but for John Rourke there was no peace as long as there was injustice. He taught survivalism, taught weapons use, taught counter-terrorist tactics. He lectured widely.

"And, to paraphrase the good Herr Doctor himself, he 'planned ahead.' Despite the periodic warmings and coolings in relations between the United States and the Soviet Union, John Rourke used all of his income not necessary for the immediate maintenance of his family to construct and stock a survival retreat in the mountains of Georgia, then one of the forty-eight contiguous states of the United States of America. When the exchange of nuclear warheads took place that fatal night, the Herr Doctor was separated from his family.

"In the intervening period between that night of terror and the dawn when the skies turned to fire, not only did Dr. Rourke locate his family and get them to safety, but he also foiled a plot by renegade forces within the Soviet government to become the only survivors on the planet . . . to destroy the returning spaceships of the Eden Project — of which we all now know — and become masters of a desolated earth.

"When, after five centuries of cryogenic sleep, the Rourke family emerged from The Retreat, there was more work to be done and John Thomas Rourke did not shirk, did not say 'Enough,' but again risked all for freedom.

"Tonight, he honors us with his presence. We intend to honor him with our highest decoration, but the two honors cannot be compared."

Could nothing save him from this? John Rourke asked himself.

Colonel Mann stepped aside and Deiter Bern reascended to the podium.

Otto Hammerschmidt's younger brother, still pale, walking with the help of a cane, was called to the podium and presented with the Knight's Cross. He declined to speak other than giving thanks. Jason Darkwood was called next and also awarded the Knight's Cross, accepting on behalf of all citizens of Mid-Wake, partners with New Germany and the other Allies for victory, for freedom.

"Dr. John Rourke."

Rourke sat in his seat, Sarah on one side of him, Natalia

on the other. Sarah prodded him, hissing, "Go on!"

"John . . . don't be bashful," Natalia whispered.

Rourke inhaled, then exhaled as he stood, buttoning his coat as he walked to the podium.

The Knight's Cross was placed around his neck and the applause rose, every man in the hall coming to his feet. The orchestra played "The Star-Spangled Banner."

John Rourke tried to step away when the National Anthem concluded, but the applause began again, continuing, not stopping. Paul was shouting, "Speech!" And John Rourke looked daggers at his friend.

The applause continued.

John Rourke looked from side to side, for once in his life praying to be rescued.

Help was not on the horizon.

He stepped forward and faced the crowd. The applause thundered on. "I'd like—" He could barely hear himself over the speaker system.

Rourke raised his arms, the palms of his hands outward.

The applause trickled off. The men sat down.

John Rourke began to speak. "As you may have detected, I'm feeling a bit uncomfortable this evening." There was some laughter, the loudest coming from Paul and Michael. He looked at them both, smiled, shook his head, then went on. "My family apparently is enjoying my discomfort. I've never been someone shy about public speaking, but I've never really been someone who felt he deserved an honor such as this, so forgive my halting attempts at thanks. I . . . uhh . . ." Rourke looked down and laughed at himself. Then he picked his head up and said, "Thank you on behalf of myself, my family . . . on behalf of all those who died fighting for the cause all of us here believe in—freedom." And he left the podium.

The applause began again, even the women standing now. Rourke seated himself, Sarah and Natalia standing on either side of him, applauding. Annie leaned over and kissed him. Paul and Michael shook his hand.

Sarah shouted over his head to Natalia. "Kiss him! I'm go-

91

ing to!" And, simultaneously, both women kissed him.

There was a shriek, a roar, and then the room began collapsing around them.

Chapter Nineteen

John grabbed for the women, Natalia's head pressed against his chest, Sarah's body hugged against him as he shielded them both. Portions of the walls were collapsing and part of the ceiling was falling down. That was the last Natalia saw as John pulled her and Sarah beneath the table, still shielding them with his own body.

Her first thought was that one of the Soviet submarine-launched missiles had struck the mountain. But if it had been nuclear, in all likelihood they would have been vaporized; or, if it had not been a direct hit, more of the structure would have been collapsing upon them. It had to have been conventional explosives, which meant it was not a missile at all. Because a conventional warhead would not have had the power to reach them this deep in the mountain that formed the center of New Germany's civilization.

They were under attack from the inside.

John had to be thinking the same thing. "It's not the Soviets, it's the damned Nazis!" he shouted over the cacophony of falling debris, screaming women, and men shouting orders all about them. In the next instant, before she could shout back to him, there was automatic weapons fire filling the hall.

Natalia tugged away from John, started to crawl along the plaster-dusted floor, her beautiful new black dress already covered with dirt. She closed her eyes, shaking her head to get some of the plaster dust out of her hair. She found what she was searching for on the floor and opened her evening bag. Crammed inside it, along with lipstick, a small hair-brush, and a handkerchief, was the Walther PPK/S, a spare magazine, and the suppressor. The suppressor was an unnecessary luxury, only the gun and the spare magazine useful to

93

her now. But if she left it, she might lose it. She twisted the suppressor onto the PKK/S's PP-length barrel, slipping the spare magazine down the front of her dress between her breasts.

More automatic weapons fire.

She peered beneath the tablecloth. A dozen men at least, in black commando gear with swastika armbands, were moving through the hall, indiscriminately spraying every table. "Bastards," she hissed.

She looked to her right. John was already in motion, the little snub-nosed .38 revolver he'd picked up at The Retreat in his right hand. Beside her, she felt a familiar presence. "Any good ideas, Michael?"

There was one of his Beretta 92F's in his left hand. "Yeah, I guess. Let's go."

As she got to a crouch beside him, she could already see Annie and Paul, guns drawn, moving off the side of the platform at the far end of the speaker's table. So far their movements had not been detected, the Nazis so methodical as they swept their way forward.

Side by side with Michael, she edged back toward the near end of the table.

Many of the round tables were overturned, officers sheltering their women behind them, those apparent few who carried arms returning fire but with little or no effect.

And then Natalia heard John's voice, "Let's get them!"

And with only the little revolver in his hand, he was running toward them.

She knew then the meaning of the expression about one's heart leaping to one's throat. . . .

Rourke found the nearest of the Nazi attackers, a man close to his own size, carrying an M16 like all the others he was able to see. "Dodd," Rourke rasped. It was the power-mad Eden Project Commander who had to be responsible for arming these men. Natalia had told him that the arms used during the attempt made on her life and Annie's could only

94

have come from the Eden Project stores.

Rourke advanced. As the black-clad Nazi assassin he'd targeted made to fire on another group of defenseless people, Rourke stepped away from the wall, the Centennial in his right hand at near-maximum extension, his right first finger drawing the trigger back until the cylinder was fully rotated and it was just ready to break. "Hey!"

The Nazi wheeled toward him, and Rourke pulled the trigger that extra fraction of an inch to strip it, the little stainless steel .38 Special bucking hard in his hand under the pressure of the Plus P load, the bridge of the killer's nose collapsing, blood spurting outward across the man's face as the Nazi fell back.

Darkwood came up in the edge of Rourke's peripheral vision, weaponless. "Grab that M16."

"Right, Doctor."

Rourke dodged left, four shots remaining in the little revolver, a single speedloader with five more rounds in an outside pocket of his tuxedo. There was pistol fire from the opposite wall. Rourke looked toward its origin, Annie and Paul engaging two of the attackers.

More debris was falling, and as Rourke looked upward for an instant, he realized the ceiling was about to completely collapse.

More of the Nazis were entering through the doors to the hall, but some of the German officers had already gotten weapons. Fighting was everywhere. Rourke reached round his back and under his coat, jerking the little A.G. Russell knife free of its sheath.

The Centennial in his right fist, the pear-shaped boot knife in his left, he started forward. A German officer was locked in combat with one of the Nazis, the latter twisting his M16 around and dealing a glancing blow to the officer with the buttstock. As the officer fell back and the Nazi turned his weapon to fire, Rourke stepped between them, firing the revolver at almost point-blank range into the Nazi's chest. The German officer grabbed for the M16 and Rourke moved on.

At the far side of his peripheral vision, he could see Natalia, the Walther in her left hand, the Bali-Song knife—she would have been carrying it in a garter on her thigh beneath her dress, he knew from experience—flashing open in her right, slashing across the throat of one of the Nazis, blood spurting everywhere around them.

John Rourke kept moving, gunfire tearing into an overturned table, the people who had tried taking shelter behind it already dead. Rourke found the source of the gunfire, firing the Centennial once, then again, spinning the Nazi assassin back on his heels and down.

Rourke wheeled right, feeling something more than any normal sensory trigger. One of the Nazis, his face twisted in rage, opened fire as Rourke threw himself left. Rourke fired, the last round in his five-shot revolver catching the Nazi high, in the mouth, the man staggering, his M16 discharging into the floor ahead of his feet, chips of floor tile and ricochets flying everywhere.

As Rourke looked right, another of the Nazis was closing in on him, swinging an M16 around toward him. Rourke dropped the revolver into an outside pocket and grabbed up a chair, flinging it at the Nazi. The chair impacted the assault rifle and the weapon fired wildly right as Rourke closed with the man, his right hand around the Nazi's throat as his left hammered forward, his fingers crushing the windpipe as his knife gouged up under the man's sternum.

Rourke pushed the man off the knife, picking up the M16.

As Rourke started to turn, another of the Nazis was bringing his weapon to bear, fewer than six feet away. There was no other choice, and Rourke's left arm arced outward, his fingers releasing the handle of the Sting IA. As the knife buried itself in the right side of the man's chest, Rourke brought the muzzle of the M16 up, the weight of the weapon convincing him that the twenty-round magazine had to have at least a few rounds left.

He punched the rifle toward the man as the Nazi struggled to raise his weapon. Rourke fired, the M16 splitting a three-round burst and emptying.

One of the Nazis was beating down a woman with the butt

of his rifle. Rourke raced the few steps toward the man, ramming the empty rifle's muzzle against his right ear, blood spurting as the Nazi screamed, then fell.

Rourke was on him now, his empty rifle fallen to the floor. Rourke's right hand closed over the revolver in his pocket, drawing and smashing it down over the Nazi's left temple, killing him.

Rourke tore the sling of the dead man's rifle free, the weapon in his right hand now as he glanced once at the woman—dead—and advanced toward the doorway. Michael, his pistol apparently empty and with no spare magazines, was using the Beretta like a bludgeon, smashing one of the Nazis over the head again and again, bringing the man down. Then Michael dropped to one knee and rose up, an M16 in his hands, firing into two more of them.

Rourke reached the doorway, a knot of Nazi personnel just on the other side, pinned down there by three German officers with captured M16's, along with Sam Aldridge.

Rourke looked back into the banquet hall. Bjorn Rolvaag, his expression almost placid-looking, was beating three of the Nazis back toward a wall with nothing more than a chair. One of the Nazis tried to raise his weapon. Rolvaag smashed the chair over the man's face, then waded in on the other two men, hammering them down with his fists.

Jason Darkwood was at the doorway now, with him Otto Hammerschmidt. A heavy volume of fire was pouring through the doorway, emanating from the Nazis stalled outside.

A stalemate, and once more John Rourke looked toward the ceiling. More and more plaster was raining down and the crack he'd noticed seconds ago was widening.

Sarah, a bloody steak knife in her right hand, Rourke's A.G. Russell knife in the other, was moving through the room, inspecting the dead and injured.

More gunfire from the Nazis on the other side of the doorway. Rourke tucked back closer to the wall beside which he stood. "Keep away from the opening!"

Inside the hall, those who could drew back.

Darkwood shouted from the other side of the doorway, "Colonel Mann took three men with him and went out through the kitchen to get behind them and—what's the term, Sam?"

"An envelopment."

Darkwood nodded. "He said give him about two minutes. I make it he's got a minute to go."

Rourke looked at the ceiling again. "Maybe we do if we're lucky." He looked at Aldridge. "Sam, get people organized to evacuate the wounded. Fast."

"Yes, sir!" and Aldridge started barking orders in the next breath.

"Hammerschmidt, help him. Get Rolvaag with you."

"Yes, Herr General!

Rourke shook his head, looking at Michael, Paul, Annie, Natalia. "Annie, Natalia, help Sarah and Maria with the injured. If someone looks too hopeless to get out, it's going to be a judgment call."

"I will make it," Natalia answered.

Rourke nodded as the woman moved off. "Michael, Paul, Jason, get us six more people who are armed. Hurry up."

Rourke was already checking the M16. Eight rounds remained in the magazine. "I need magazines!" Rourke shouted to anyone within hearing range. He let the M16 fall to his side on its sling, taking the bloodied revolver from the pocket of the ruined tuxedo, his thumb pushing forward on the cylinder release catch, his trigger finger pushing the cylinder out of the frame. He let the revolver roll back in his hand, nesting it between his thumb and little finger, sliding his thumb up over the frame and punching the ejector rod downward, spilling the empty brass to the plaster-covered floor between his feet.

He took the speedloader from his pocket as he righted the revolver, started the five rounds into the five charging holes, and let the loader activate against the ejector star, all five rounds chambering simultaneously. As his left hand pocketed the empty loader for later use, his right thumb swung the cylinder closed and rotated it slightly left and down, indexing it.

He dropped the revolver into his waistband just left of his navel.

A young German officer ran up, handed him seemingly filled twenty-round magazines. "These are all that I could find, Herr Doctor General."

Rourke smiled, shook his head, and put one of the three twenties up the well of the M16, keeping the one with eight rounds as a spare, then handing around the other two magazines.

The ceiling would go at any second.

Rourke shouted back, "As soon as we're into the corridor, start evacuating as quickly as possible!"

And he looked at Michael, Paul, and Jason Darkwood. Darkwood had six other men. All nine were armed with M16's. Paul had his battered old Browning High Power in his left hand, the hammer down.

"You and you." Rourke picked two of the men at random. "Understand enough English?" he asked perfunctorily. They both indicated they did. "Good. I want suppressive fire on the Nazi position." Han Lu Chen, the Chinese intelligence agent from the First City, approached, M16 in hand. Rourke nodded to him, then continued. "Nice controlled bursts, firing high and low, alternating so they'll think there are more than just two of you. Keep firing until you've each fired three bursts, then cease fire until we're through the doors and on them. Then join us, right?"

"Yes, Herr Doctor General," the senior of the two men—boys—acknowledged.

"Take up your positions. Paul, Michael, stick with me. You too, Han. Jason, take the rest of them."

Darkwood grinned, "Yes, Herr Doctor General."

"Blow it your ear," Rourke grinned back.

Flanking the door on either side, the two young Germans who were to provide the suppressive fire were in position. In almost perfect synchronization, the two officers opened fire, neat three- and four-round bursts in a crossfire pattern against the Nazi position beyond the large double doors of

99

the banquet hall.

The ceiling above John Rourke was groaning loudly now, about to collapse.

As the German officers snapped their rifles up, Rourke shouted the first word that came to mind, "Charge!"

His twice-liberated M16 firing in short, full auto bursts, Michael and Paul flanking him, Rourke raced through the space between the doors.

The Nazis were positioned just inside the doors of the hall in which the dance was being held, the room still brightly lit and decorated with banners featuring both the German and United States colors.

Rourke and the others with him sprinted across the corridor, a grenade hurled toward them. Rourke wheeled toward it, shouting, "Out of the way!" and took one of the greatest risks he'd ever taken. He kicked the grenade as hard as he could, sending it arcing down the corridor in mid-air as it exploded. Gunfire tore past him and into the floor near his feet.

Michael and Paul were the first two through the doorway, Michael taking a hit, going down, firing, then getting back on his feet. Rourke's rifle had eight rounds remaining in the magazine and he threw the selector to semi-auto, firing a single shot into the chest of one of the Nazis, wheeling a few degrees left, then firing a second round into the head of another. As he tried for a third shot, one of the Nazis threw himself at Rourke, deflecting the M16. The third shot went wild, Rourke and the man falling to the floor.

The man was powerfully built, his hands enormous, closing around Rourke's throat. John Rourke's right knee smashed up, missing the groin, striking the pelvis. But his right hand got free enough to reach for the Centennial inside the waistband of his trousers. With the muzzle flush against the man's testicles, Rourke fired, the recoil nearly snapping his own right wrist.

Rourke pushed the man away, then fired a second shot into the Nazi's head as he got to one knee.

His M16 gone, Rourke had only the revolver. He fired,

hitting another of the Nazis in the left side of the neck. Paul was butt-stroking one of the Nazis as the man fell, twisting the pistol from his grasp. "John!"

The pistol—a Beretta 92F—sailed from Paul's hand. Rourke caught it, stepping back, firing the last two rounds from his revolver into the chest of a Nazi turning toward him with an M16.

Rourke turned the Beretta in his left hand, worked the safety off, and double actioned another round into the Nazi's throat.

Michael, his left arm bleeding, was locked in combat with two of the Nazis.

Rourke jumped a dead body, smashed the butt of the Centennial down across the neck of one of them, then fired a point-blank double tap from the Beretta into the chest of the second man.

Michael shouted, "Thanks," stabbed the Beretta that was in his right hand toward another of the Nazis, and fired, killing the man.

Rourke caught up an M16 as he dropped the Centennial into his pocket, the Colt assault rifle in his right fist, the Beretta 92F in his left. Rourke fired into a knot of Nazis trying to escape toward the rear of the hall, cutting down three of them, wounding a fourth.

From the opposite side of the corridor, there was a tremendous crash, the floor beneath Rourke's feet vibrating with it.

One of the Nazis, shot through several times it appeared and close to death, reached up from the floor near Rourke's feet.

John Rourke put a burst from the rifle into the man's head.

A cloud of plaster dust belched across the corridor and through the doors into the ballroom, dense as heavy fog. John Rourke held his breath against it, the fighting here all but done.

He ran into the corridor, chunks of the ceiling collapsing around him.

He could hear Wolfgang Mann's voice shouting over the din, saying, "Kleinermann, assist in subduing the enemy personnel in the ballroom. The rest of you, to the banquet hall!"

Men were everywhere around Rourke now as he coughed and choked, at last penetrating the cloud of dust inside the banquet hall. Chunks of the ceiling, enormous in size, lay everywhere. All about him were the moans of the injured and dying.

Rourke handed off his rifle.

His skills as a doctor were needed now more than anything else.

Chapter Twenty

Sarah assisted one of the German doctors at an aid station set up in the far end of the ballroom, as distant as possible from the still-unstable ceiling of the banquet hall and the almost as badly damaged corridor. Natalia, Annie, and Maria helped at another aid station at the far end of the corridor, where there was no evidence of immediate structural damage. Michael, his left arm stiff at his side, the sleeve of his jacket cut away and a blood-stained bandage over his bicep, joined Rourke and Paul Rubenstein.

John Rourke, in his shirtsleeves now, the partially loaded Beretta in his trouser band beside the fully emptied Smith & Wesson revolver, crossed into the corridor once more. Flanked by his son and his friend, he clambered over the debris and toward the center of the banquet hall, where people were still buried alive.

Darkwood called to them from the still-thick clouds of plaster dust, more falling by the second. "John! I've got one that's alive!"

Rourke spat dust from his mouth, calling back into the corridor, "Tell Colonel Mann we need those gas masks quickly."

As they reached Darkwood, kneeling atop a pile of debris, Sam Aldridge appeared from inside the mound, his black hair washed grey with dust, his uniform torn. And Aldridge was coughing badly. "Got a woman down there, Doctor . . . she's . . ." Aldridge began coughing so badly he could not speak.

Rourke looked at Darkwood, who was coughing, too. "Jason, you get Sam out of here, and yourself, too. Get some fresh air and stay out of here until we've got masks. Make sure they're all checked for filters. Now, get outa here."

Darkwood nodded, coughed, tried to speak. He hauled Sam Aldridge's right arm across his shoulders and started helping the black marine captain down the mound of debris toward the doors.

"Let me go," Paul volunteered. "I'm smaller."

Rourke looked at his friend and nodded. Logic was logic.

Paul handed Michael his High Power and dropped to his knees, then started into the hole, shouting downward, "I'm coming to help you out of there, ma'am."

John Rourke looked around them as his friend disappeared down inside the hole. The speakers' table where they had all sat less than fifteen minutes ago was all but buried, the dais on which it had been set collapsed. The podium was partially buried and lay on the floor on its side. As far as could be told in these first moments after the disaster, no one that he knew more than casually was unaccounted for, but that could change at any moment.

Paul shouted up. "John?"

Rourke leaned over the hole, Michael beside him. It was darker inside than he'd expected and he had no flashlight. "What is it? How is she?"

"She might have a broken back; I'm not sure."

"I'm coming down." Rourke handed Michael the Beretta, "Here, take this, and this, too," he said, passing his son the little revolver as well. Rourke's bowtie was already undone, and he ripped it from beneath his collar now. His hands, which were only partially healed, were already cracking and bleeding in spots from the abrasive action of the plaster. He placed one hand on either side of the hole and started to let himself down.

The hole's interior diameter was tight, almost too tight for his shoulders. He reached the bottom in a second or so, going into a crouch. He could barely see and the plaster dust was chokingly thick. Ahead of him, he could hear Paul coughing. He started on hands and knees toward the sound. To have fired the Zippo lighter in his trouser pocket for illumination could have been suicidal. With the heavy

104

concentration of dust, he had no reason to suspect it would not be combustible.

"John!"

In a moment Rourke was on his knees, stooped over beside Paul Rubenstein. In the poor light Rourke could make out the woman's gross features, but nothing in detail. And, he reminded himself, he had better vision in poor light than most people, the concurrent upside to his always inordinate light sensitivity.

Rourke coughed, nearly choking as he bent over the woman, his hands moving along her body. As he stopped coughing enough to speak, he asked, "Paul, what made you think—" And then John Rourke answered his own question. The woman's body was twisted at the waist at an unnatural angle. She was breathing, but heavily. His hand traveled down her left leg and he pinched it. The woman groaned. There was feeling. With greater difficulty, he got his hands beneath her, feeling along her spine. "It's not broken. But she does have broken ribs, and likely there's a fracture in one or both legs the way they're twisted." Rourke coughed again; Paul was also choking. "You get out of here. Get the Germans to haul in some of that heavy equipment they're promising."

"They were saying they weren't certain the floor would take it." Paul began another coughing spasm.

Rourke held back the cough he felt rising in his throat. "Get them to evacuate anything below us in this building, get a move on with any of the other more easily moved casualties. We'll need that guest list checked and verified for attendance. Once we've got a count, then bring in the equipment. In the meantime, I'll need oxygen down here for her and a gas mask for myself. Find one of the other doctors and get him down here ready for a glucose I.V. to keep her going until we get her out of here."

"All right . . . I'll . . ." Paul was seized by a fit of coughing again.

"I know; you'll be back quickly."

"Right!" Paul coughed, squeezed past him, and was

gone.

Rourke found the woman's hand and held it, speaking to her softly in German between coughing spasms. She was coughing. Rourke could do nothing for her. He had his A.G. Russell Sting IA Black Chrome back, so if he'd had something to use as a tube, he could have eased the woman's breathing with a tracheostomy if that were necessary, but he couldn't even do that.

He kept holding her hand, telling her that everything would be all right soon, that she'd suffered no permanent damage — he hoped — and no disfigurement, something he'd learned to do with female patients back in his emergency room days just out of school, which was a vital reassurance.

And he waited.

Chapter Twenty-one

One of the Nazis was under the doctor's knife now. Natalia watched the German doctor's eyes over the rims of his eyeglasses. "The bastard has a bullet so close to his heart . . . I should not try this."

Natalia looked at him. "If you wait, he will die."

"If I try to get that bullet out, he could die, too."

"That's why they call you a physician. What can I do to help?"

The young doctor looked at her.

"Damn you, Fräulein," he whispered, then began to roll up his sleeves.

Natalia smiled as a thought crossed her mind. In her ruined evening gown, she had no sleeves to roll. . . .

"Close him, nurse."

She hadn't been addressed by that title for five centuries. Sarah Rourke looked at the doctor whom she assisted. He was an older man, appearing to be past retirement age, but his hands had been steady when he removed the bullet from the young Chinese officer's neck. He was already turning to the next patient, too, so she had no choice.

She began closing the wound.

"You were very good, Frau Rourke," the old man called to her, then turned to his new patient.

Sarah Rourke's back was killing her from standing, even though she'd kicked off her already-low-heeled shoes. She shook her head, keeping at the suturing. . . .

John Rourke emerged from the hole, Michael helping

him out. Through the mask, Michael's voice sounded odd, hollow. "You all right, Dad?"

John Rourke nodded. His back ached from being bent over for so long and, despite the mask, he still coughed, an unnerving enough experience in itself inside the gas mask.

The blocks and tackle were already nearly set. From inside the hole, the young German doctor who had replaced him a few moments ago shouted, "I am staying down here with her while the hole is opened. I cannot leave her alone."

John Rourke looked into the darkness below and thought, "Good man."

Chapter Twenty-two

It was four in the morning New Germany time and he was exhausted, but the canned air of the city would not suffice for him now.

In his plaster-coated black trousers and dirt-stained white shirt, his jacket hooked over his shoulder and one of the captured Berettas in his waistband, John Rourke left the hospital where he had been working nearly nonstop for the last six hours. He had saved some lives but been unable to save others. Such was the physician's perennial lament, and he wondered as he walked whether or not that, just as much as other reasons, had been why he'd left medicine in the first place.

He wanted to smoke a cigar, wanted to very much. But to smoke would have been counterproductive, since the purpose of his walk was to get fresh air. Military personnel were everywhere despite the hour, reserve units called up by Wolfgang Mann. And latest word had it that calling up the reserves was not at all unwarranted, nor was it premature. The Soviet submarine fleet was no longer merely on station but was maneuvering off the coast. Soviet presence in the Falkland Islands, a staging area used by the Soviet Forces for the past several weeks, was increasing by the hour.

Rourke neared the main entrance, the enormous blast doors closed and secured. He approached the young first lieutenant who had the guard. The man saluted, "Herr Doctor General!"

"At ease. I'd just like to use the little access door over there and go outside for a breath of fresh air."

"But, Herr Doctor General! It would be very dangerous to do and—"

"Lieutenant, isn't there a considerable presence of the

forces of New Germany on the other side of those doors? Armor, infantry, even Long Range Mountain Patrol units?"

"Yes, Herr Doctor General, but—"

"Then how could I be any safer? Open the door, and please listen when I knock to return. Should we have a code knock?"

"I will—I will be able to see you, Herr Doctor General, on the video monitoring system."

"See, I'll be safe as church."

"As—"

"As church. Church, synagogue, temple, mosque . . . all means to the same end."

"To the same end, Herr Doctor General?"

"Yes. I'll pass through that access doorway now, please."

"Yes, Herr Doctor General!" And the young man saluted.

Rourke nodded.

He followed the man toward the doorway, and the young officer directed his subordinates—of which there were many—to open the door so the Herr Doctor General could pass. Rourke was beginning to worry that this title, ungainly and embarrassing as it was, might stick.

Then, at last, as he stepped over the flange and into the night, he could breathe proper air again. As he filled his lungs with it, he experienced an almost giddy sensation. It was cool, impossibly fresh and, because of the jungle vegetation so near, heady by comparison.

And he realized that he had not been so starved for real air, he would likely have sniffed synth-fuel residue, because outside the blast doors that protected the interior, German armor and other vehicles were everywhere.

The German armor was very good, highly mobile, fast, but so vastly smaller than the Soviet armor that Rourke doubted the German war machines would have much of a chance against their Soviet counterparts.

The battle which, for some time, John Rourke had considered inevitable, was nearly at hand.

As a boy, because it was there and deserved to be experienced, he had read the Bible in the King James Version. He recalled now, "And he gathered them together into a place called in the Hebrew tongue Armageddon."

Enough fresh air consumed, he decided he could have that cigar now. He removed one from an interior breast pocket of his coat, the tip already excised as was his custom. He lit the cigar in the blue-yellow flame of his battered Zippo, inhaled the smoke slowly into his lungs, flicked the lighter's cowling closed, then dropped it into his pocket.

As he exhaled, he began to walk, officers passing him, saluting him, Rourke nodding in return. He'd never been a military man and would not affect that he had.

At any moment, the sky would rain death.

He knew that.

And, so, he enjoyed the moment of quiet and peace like that exquisitely rare and wonderful thing that it was.

There might never be another.

Chapter Twenty-three

The air raid sirens did not waken him as much as Sarah's movement in bed beside him. "John?"

He sat bolt upright, his right arm around her, his left hand pressed against her abdomen. He kissed her lightly, then hard on the mouth.

The telephone beside the bed rang.

He let it ring, holding her.

Finally, Sarah reached for it. "Yes, Wolf. He's here."

Rourke squinted as Sarah turned on the light and the grey darkness dissolved into a yellow wash. He was very tired. "Colonel?"

Mann sounded as tired as Rourke felt. Rourke looked at the Rolex Submariner on his wrist. He'd gotten to bed at five. It was almost, but not quite, two hours later than that. "The Soviet Fleet off our coast has ceased movement. Bombardment seems imminent."

"Where can Sarah go for safety?"

"John!"

"Don't argue."

"John?"

"No . . . not you, Colonel."

"There is the bunker built by the Leader some years ago. It is several levels underground and well stocked. Dieter Bern goes there now."

"Send a small unit for my wife, my daughter, Dr. Leuden, and Major Tiemerovna."

"John!"

Rourke looked at his wife, held her close. "Where should I join you, Colonel? It'll take me about five minutes."

"I will send a driver along with the personnel to accompany your wife."

"Very good. You'll contact Michael and Paul, then. See you shortly."

Rourke handed his wife the telephone receiver.

She hung it up.

"Go ahead," Rourke told his wife. "Tell me how a woman who's pregnant should be out there at the front, wherever the hell that'll be."

"John . . . I love you."

"I know." And John Rourke drew his wife's body against him. Why wasn't there ever time? He held her, telling himself, as each second passed, just one second more. . . .

Michael Rourke slipped his feet over the side of the bed and stared at them under the wash of light from the lamp.

Maria put her arms around his neck, her face against his back. "I want to be with you, Michael."

"You can't."

"I won't get in the way!"

"I didn't say that you'd get in the way. But I just want you safe, that's all."

Michael tried to stand up, but she held him more tightly. "If you die, I want to die, too."

"Maria, I'm not going to die." His left arm ached, felt stiff, and the left cheek of his butt hurt from the tetanus/antibiotic cocktail with which he'd been injected. "I'll function better knowing that you're safe. Colonel Mann said that Natalia and Annie and my mother would be with you, taken to safety. That's where you belong."

Maria began to cry.

Michael started to get dressed. . . .

There was no time for a shower, and he'd showered less than two hours ago, anyway, so John Rourke merely stood under the water, trying to come fully awake. He'd survived on less sleep and likely would again. And, en route to the coast, he might be able to grab a few winks, he hoped.

Sarah was talking to him, and from the sound of her voice he could tell she was brushing her teeth. "Can I get anything out for you, John?"

"A pair of black BDU pants, one of those black knit pullover shirts, socks, underpants . . . like that."

"Take a sweater?"

"Sure. Sarah?"

"Yes?"

"I love you."

"I know that," his wife told him. . . .

Annie stormed, "Being a woman is perfectly fine, but the way men perceive women sucks."

"Annie," Paul tried to counter, half into his pants, just looking at her. "I can't—"

She was stepping into a slip and pulled it up to her waist, then looked at him. "It's Daddy, isn't it?"

"What do you mean?"

"I should be beside you and we both know that, but Daddy thinks—"

"Annie, for God's sake! I want you with me, but I love you too much to put you into—"

"—danger? Be real, Paul."

Paul finally had his pants up. "I don't—"

"—know what to say?" And she came into his arms, her own arms going around his neck and kissed him hard on the mouth. "I love you and I'll obey you, but the obey part doesn't mean I have to like it, or I forfeit my right to bitch."

"Ohh . . ."

And he held her so tightly she started to laugh, then said in a throaty voice he could almost taste, "I can't breathe!"

He kissed her. . . .

John Rourke had the taste of Sarah still on his lips, the feel of her on the flesh of his hands.

The door opened.

114

In one of her black jumpsuits, her revolvers buckled to her waist, Natalia Anastasia Tiemerovna just stood there. "This is your doing, isn't it?"

"Yes."

"I am not someone to be shunted off and—"

"Yes, you are. If you should die, I'd—"

"What, John?"

"Damnit." John Rourke turned and walked away. Colonel Mann's driver and the security unit that would usher the women to the bunker were already coming up the corridor.

Chapter Twenty-four

John Rourke had planned ahead.

A south wind shrieked across the landing pad set atop the mountain, lashing men and aircraft with a strength that was almost humanly vicious. Sets of lift tubes were positioned at the four cardinal points and men of the Allied commando force spilled from them, running, heavily laden with weapons and gear, toward their waiting aircraft. Within minutes, the aircraft would be airborne and more aircraft would take their place, and more men would hurry toward them, fill their fuselages, and the process would cycle through again.

Rourke had his face turned into the wind, relishing its freshness, his eyes still burning from lack of sleep. And he would need alertness. He turned his head to the right. The sun was still low on the horizon.

Colonel Mann approached, accompanying Jason Darkwood. Rourke massaged his hands as he looked away, then back toward them. There was the low whine of another J7-V taking off vertically, then reorienting and streaking away toward the east.

Over the sounds of aircraft, and the booted feet and softly clinking equipment of running Allied Commandoes, Wolfgang Mann said, "Field Intelligence indicates a large Soviet force is positioning itself for attack on the Complex, John. We have very little time."

Rourke only nodded.

Jason Darkwood said, "If we're successful in achieving our objective, Colonel, any Soviet ground attack can be all but neutralized."

"And, if we are not," John Rourke almost whispered. . . .

116

Natalia—perhaps the tight black jumpsuit she wore enhancing that image, Sarah thought—paced like a caged cat. Sarah Rourke looked from Natalia to Annie. Annie stood by the bunker doors, rocking on her boot heels. As she rocked, her skirt swayed in rhythm to her motion, back and forth. Sarah dug her hands into the pockets of her BDU pants and looked down at her body. The BDU blouse was very fully cut, but her abdomen was very fully swollen. And, over her abdomen's greatest extension, the closures were very tightly stretched.

She walked across the room. It was actually more like a cave above their heads, at the very edge of upward penetration of the light. The highest point of the ceiling was perhaps sixty feet overhead, but a mere twelve feet overhead was stretched an interlocking network of beams, similar beams rising from the floor to meet them, the floor really a platform set over the cave floor itself. The platform, its perimeter defined by these upthrusting beams, was like a vast proscenium stage.

As she reached the nearest of the edges, she looked down. The cave floor was some six feet below, and when she craned her neck, she could just make out support beams beneath the platform. These, like the beams crossing overhead and those rising out of the platform itself to mate with the overheads, were all fitted with devices resembling huge automobile shock absorbers like those she'd seen five centuries ago in late night TV commercials when waiting up for John to return home.

She had read, in science magazines of the period, about the work being done to earthquake-proof skyscrapers and public buildings. And, indeed, it seemed as if this platform that formed the living and working area within the bunker was constructed to withstand all but direct collapse of the granite cave surrounding them, regardless of what the earth beneath them should do.

117

She looked back along the platform. And she could see, very well defined, the partitioned-off living quarters, office space, storage areas, and the like. There was more storage, the young German officer who had accompanied them had recounted, this deeper within the bowels of the cave itself, these storage areas laser cut from the living rock. Food, water, medical supplies, weapons, and ammunition . . . everything necessary to survive for an extremely protracted period of time without ever returning to the surface. Air scrubbers, as well as a small greenhouse area under artificial lights, would keep the oxygen supply fresh.

It was so much like The Retreat, she suddenly realized, and maybe that was why she shivered here. . . .

John Rourke pulled on the trouser portion of the one-piece dry suit, already wearing the issue black Mid-Wake surface suit beneath it. The J7-V flew onward toward the coast. In less than fifteen minutes, they would be bailing out, joining personnel already on the ground.

Rourke stood up, taking the double Alessi shoulder rig with its twin stainless Detonics pistols from the seat beside him, shouldering into it. The little stainless autoloaders were chamber empty now, as was his custom with a Colt/Browning style auto during an air drop. Without removing the guns from the leather, one at a time he pulled the magazines, checked that they each carried six rounds, then reinserted them up the butts. Clipped into one of the pockets of the surface suit was the little A.G. Russell Sting IA Black Chrome. Rourke now pulled the dry suit the rest of the way up, over the surface suit's integral SAS-style leg holster, one of the Detonics Scoremaster's secured there. The second Scoremaster was in a water- and pressure-proof pouch in the small pack he would don with his underwater gear. No room this time for his revolver, what additional room there was taken up by spare magazines for his pistols.

He pulled the dry suit all the way up, closing it at his throat and rolling over the collar.

Around his waist, he secured the Mid-Wake issue combat belt, a Soviet STY-20 dart gun on one side, his fighting knife on the other, various medical and survival and repair pouches attached across the back and front. He carried his Crain Life Support System X knife with the twelve-inch blade in the sheath he'd had fabricated for him at Mid-Wake, the sheath made from the same material as the ones Darkwood and the other Mid-Wake personnel used for their own knives, many of these custom knives like his own.

Darkwood's knife was of particular interest, Rourke thought, an identical duplicate of the Randall Smithsonian Bowie Darkwood's ancestor had brought to Mid-Wake five centuries ago, the original on display at the New Smithsonian at Mid-Wake.

Rourke looked across to the opposite side of the fuselage where Paul and Michael geared up. Each checked the other's equipment. As Rourke started into his, Jason Darkwood came up, offering, "We can check each other, Doctor."

"Fine."

Darkwood nodded, picking up Rourke's kit. "I know this in theory, but frankly, jumping out of one of these flying machines scares the shit out of me."

"It's never something one becomes easily used to, Jason. Parachuting can be fun when the purpose is fun. When one's bailing out into combat, on the plus side, there can be more serious considerations." And Rourke smiled. "The enemy can always shoot you out of the sky."

"Ohh, boy," Darkwood grinned, Rourke looking at him over his shoulder. "I suppose you're as at home falling through the sky as I am underwater."

Rourke shrugged his shoulders, but not in response to Darkwood's remark, merely to better settle his harness.

119

The parachutes were jury-rigged by the Germans to accommodate the necessity to quickly, almost instantly, move out underwater. Because of that, the standard German parachute harnesses were coupled to the standard Mid-Wake underwater gear, but the parachute packs quickly separable, each compensated for negative bouyancy, so the discarded chute and attendant packs would sink to the bottom as rapidly as possible.

The individual components were as tested and reliable as could be possible for battle gear, but they had never been used before in tandem.

"Your wings seem secure," Darkwood told Rourke. "Is everybody certain the covering will break away when we drop the parachutes?"

"Theoretically," Rourke smiled.

"Yes, theoretically," Darkwood groaned. . . .

They stood by the open fuselage door.

John Rourke looked down the line behind him. Paul. Michael. Darkwood. Aldridge. Han Lu Chen of the First Chinese City. Otto Hammerschmidt. There were ten other men, five of them like Hammerschmidt, German Long Range Mountain Patrol or Commando, the remaining five United States Marine Corps from Mid-Wake.

Of the sixteen men waiting in the doorway behind John Rourke aside from Rourke himself, only Hammerschmidt and his five men were experienced jumpers, and only Rourke among them had ever bailed out over water.

Rourke held to the straps and leaned out a little to peer through the open fuselage doorway. The cloud layer through which they flew parted here and there, and beneath that, the ocean far below seemed still. But, unless the German intelligence data was wrong, beneath the surface lay an undisclosed number of Island Class submarines of the Soviet Fleet. And in hours—unlikely—in minutes, or even in seconds, the Island Classers would launch their missiles against the Capitol of New Germany and a fourth World War would begin in earnest, or the Third World War would end.

Chapter Twenty-five

Annie Rourke Rubenstein sat at the farthest interior edge of the platform, her feet over the side, swinging. When she swung them back, she could not see them because the hem of her skirt flared outward slightly, and when she swung them forward, she watched them intensely.

What was she doing here?

Her husband, her father, her brother, and her many friends — because they were men, they were outside of this granite coccoon, preparing to fight or fighting already, trying not to die but perhaps dying already.

And because she was female, she was here, in as much safety as they could provide.

Women were physically smaller, of course, or usually so, at least. And, all things being equal, they were possessed of less upper body strength. Generally, men could run faster.

She had never wished to be a man, always quite content with her womanhood, more so — ohh, so much more so — since becoming Paul's wife. But she was never content with the idea men had about women, that they were to be excluded.

She pulled her feet up and turned around, bringing her knees almost to her chin.

There were no men here.

There was not a single one.

Only wives of high-ranking officers, the daughters of those wives, the female relatives of the political elite, and a number of female German military personnel, presumably to assist the female civilians or perhaps to guard them in the remotely possible event of the mountain's being over-

run and the vault doors sealing them inside somehow occurring.

Aside from these female military personnel, Annie, her
mother, and Natalia were the only persons who were
armed.

She could see her mother sitting down, her pistol belt
across her lap. Her mother sat down a great deal these
days . . . the baby, of course. She could see Natalia pacing
back and forth, smoking a cigarette, angry looks being
fired at her because she was 'polluting' the scrubbed air.

Annie Rourke Rubenstein recalled the lines from John
Milton: "Thousands at his bidding speed, And post o'er
land and ocean without rest; They also serve who only
stand and wait."

She wasn't standing, and she was, already, damned tired
of waiting.

Chapter Twenty-six

Darkwood looked at the dual display on the face of his Steinmetz chronometer. There was absolutely no reason in the world to want or need to know the time just now. His world was circumscribed by an open doorway in the belly of a flying machine thousands of feet over the water.

Whatever time it was in New Germany or in Mid-Wake or anywhere else was of absolutely no concern.

He supposed he studied the face of his watch because it was a familiar face. Sam Aldridge, Dr. Rourke, Paul Rubenstein, Michael Rourke—none of their faces could he really see. Each of them, like himself and all the others, was helmeted, effectively masked from familiar recognition. suited up, ready to throw body and soul into the air and plummet toward the ocean's surface.

The ocean itself was unfamiliar to him. He had logged innumerable—or so it seemed—thousands of miles in the service of his country, but at no time had such service taken him out of the world's largest ocean, the Pacific.

Water was water, salinity salinity.

Poets—and scientists to a degree—spoke of the waters of the ocean and the liquid content of the human body being alike. The poets pondered its significance, philosophized over the hidden meaning, while the scientists . . . What did the scientists do? They drew conclusions, of course, but only tentative ones because each mystery unraveled only led to another mystery still to be solved.

In the five centuries since the fall of old surface earth, neither poets nor scientists had solved very much. And, in their way, both poets and scientists were philosophers. Men and women and children still died. Wars were still fought.

The sea took back its own, and if blood and seawater held so much in common, in the end, then, they became indistinguishable one from the other.

In the fuselage doorway, John Rourke called out through their headset receivers, "Be ready!"

Jason Darkwood studied the light over the door.

The light—still red—was unfamiliar, although he knew its purpose. Aboard this vessel, the *Reagan*, a shift to red meant that night vision was to be preserved for likely surfacing. Here, a shift to green meant that all one's past and all one's future would rest on how well packed was a piece of flimsy-seeming cloth called a parachute.

And, there were even holes in this terrifying thing, intentionally placed there. What if the holes were in the wrong spots, or there were just too many of them? He had been told from the first, when he had pushed to be released prematurely from medical treatment and to come along on this mission, that parachuting was quite routine. And he'd also known that, without him, assuming the first phase of the mission were successful, neither the second nor third phase held any real hope for success. This realization was not the fantasy of ego, although ego was good and necessary, but arose from an objective evaluation of their task.

The business about parachutes was roughly the same sort of thing they'd told him at the Academy the first time he'd put on wings and a hemosponge and gone out of an airlock.

And, after a time, survival and day-to-day activity in the water became routine.

But there were backups, things one could do underwater that one could not do, Darkwood imagined, while falling out of an aircraft.

He'd asked John Rourke, "Doctor, what do I do—besides die, I mean—should my primary chute fail and my secondary chute fail?"

"It all depends, Jason."

"On what, sir?"

"On how resourceful you are, how able to overcome fear sufficiently to act."

"But what action is appropriate?"

"Why don't you guess, and then I'll tell you if you're right."

That had seemed fair enough certainly, and Darkwood carefully considered his response. But then Dr. Rourke clapped his hands together loudly. "What is it, Doctor?"

"I was just simulating the sound of your body impacting a hard surface without an open chute. A falling body accelerates at a speed of thirty-two feet per second per second, of course, and the initial height would—"

"I took too long?"

"You took too long."

"So, assuming I bounced, how do I get my chute open?"

Dr. Rourke laughed then, lighting one of his cigars. "What would you do if your equipment malfunctioned underwater?"

Darkwood smiled, saying, "Well, fix it, of course."

"Right. The problem with a parachute isn't usually the chute itself. Either it won't open at all or at least not properly or, when it does, it becomes tangled up. In the latter case, if there's time, cut away your primary chute if you think you'll need to. It'll give you something else to think about until you hit."

"And in the former case?"

"Manually start the chute, but in such a way that you don't mutilate it or tangle it."

"It sounds like dying is simpler."

"Well, it happens more often," Dr. Rourke told him.

Jason Darkwood touched at the Smithsonian Bowie now. At least he could try. . . .

The light went green. "Geronimo!" He vanished from the doorway.

Why had his father, an eminently sensible man, shouted such an inane expression? Because thousands of other men had shouted it as they dove out of airplanes?

He thought of a better thing to say. "Shit!"

Ahead of him, Paul shouted the same thing—"Geronimo!"—then jumped.

Michael Rourke approached the doorway, his eyes on the light. It would be red for at least . . .

It went green.

He jumped.

"Shi—i—i—i—i—it!"

He felt like an idiot.

He shut off his radio, as per instructions. But now Michael Rourke was spinning and he knew he shouldn't be spinning. Then he remembered to stop shouting into his helmet and deafening himself, and to use his arms and legs to stabilize himself.

It would have been worse if it were night, because now at least he could see some of the others coming after him through the doorway. His body twisted and then he could see nothing but the whiteness of the clouds all around him, couldn't see his father, couldn't see Paul, either.

And then he was through, the clouds like low-lying fog, and suddenly he reached a crest of ground. But instead of lying below him, it stretched above him.

Below him he saw his father and his friend. They were so near that if he had been able to maneuver halfway decently, Michael told himself, he could have reached out and touched them, linked hands like he'd seen skydivers doing in videos at The Retreat.

His chest pack.

He remembered to look at it. Plenty of altitude remained according to the digital altimeters, which were in perfect synchronization. There was plenty of time before he'd have to open a chute. He was falling, but so remarkably slowly he realized he was smiling, enjoying the sensations. How wonderful it would have been to do this without every square centimeter of his body being covered.

Euphoria.

That was what it was. The German sergeant with the

stumbling English—however halting, vastly better than Michael's still-meager German—had told them, "When in the air dropping through there is sometimes the feeling in English called as euphoria—mispronounced—whereby the parachute-dropping man is much very excited and does not his own descent control happens."

On one level of consciousness, Michael Rourke realized he was no longer thinking clearly. But God, it was so beautiful and so free, like the birds he remembered from his childhood. And he felt tears rising in his eyes, for the birds, for all of them, except that the comparative few the Germans had released and those meager numbers in zoological confinement were gone forever.

He saw his father, or was it Paul?

Normally, the height discrepancy would have been dead . . .

Dead, Michael Rourke thought.

Euphoria.

Euphoria had been making love with Madison, his once and forever wife. And if he were dead, and what he'd been taught as a child, sometimes questioning but sincerely wanting to believe were true, when he was dead, he would be reunited with her, see their child.

Did dead people see?

Would their child forever be a child, or were all spirits one age and therefore ageless?

His eyes drifted over the water.

How lovely it was!

Peaceful.

And how beautiful were the chutes opening above him.

"Above me," he murmured inside his helmet. "Above me? Above me!"

His eyes shifted to the two altimeters. He was almost . . . Michael Rourke triggered his primary chute, the main chute blossoming above him, jerking him upward, sucking the breath from him for a moment, the smaller chute out, the lines surrounding him suddenly stiff.

His hands reached up; his eyes looked downward. The

surface was rushing away, slowed, just seemed to hang below him, and then he started tugging at the lines as he'd been instructed to do, to guide his descent as the water rose to meet him.

Already, one of the chutes was on the water, under the water, and gone. A second chute.

Michael Rourke's feet hit the water, and he seemed to fall forward into it as a wave crashed over him and down, down he fell. He tapped at the quick release fixture for the parachute harness, but then suddenly he was suffocating. He was rolling, thrashing. . . .

And he activated the controls for the hemosponge and his helmet systems came alive. The wings he'd never tried folded open from his back and he moved through the water, like a bird on the air.

Chapter Twenty-seven

John Rourke was grateful for the time he'd allocated to learn the diving systems of Mid-Wake, grateful because the experience had been at once enlightening and enjoyable, and grateful now because he felt nearly at home as his wings furled and unfurled and he glided through the water, hovering there, his wings beating gently, the air processed by his hemosponge fresh-tasting enough, his body warm but pleasantly so in his black dry suit, all helmet systems operational.

He switched to vision intensification, and fewer than fifty feet below the surface, the difference was so instantly pronounced that his eyes automatically squinted against the light.

The sea was life, he realized.

Because, unlike the land, all around there was life in abundance. Two Atlantic bluntnose jacks, both large for the species, about a foot in length, swam past him, golden yellow, their second dorsal fins quivering. His eyes followed them and he was startled when, at the far left corner of his peripheral vision, something moved snakelike toward him. As his hand reached for the Crain LS-X, his wings fluttering to draw him back, Rourke smiled. The silvery creature was merely a cutlassfish.

Paul moved through the water toward him, another jack giving the younger man a wide berth.

From above, wings moving erratically still, Rourke saw his son. And, in the next instant, the surface was as alive as if a school of sharks were feeding, parachute packs sinking downward toward the ocean floor as wings unfurled and black helmeted men, Sty-20 pistols in their hands, swam downward.

130

John Rourke signaled with his hands, and the translucent-winged men of the attack force floated through the water toward him.

Darkwood. Darkwood tipped his helmet against Rourke's own and Rourke could hear his voice. "I'm home, Doctor. The parachute ride wasn't that bad, but I'll take the water over the air any day."

John Rourke answered saying, "You have a beautiful world. If we're successful, perhaps your people will someday be able to benefit from its full potential."

Darkwood seemed about to speak, but then Paul joined them, touched helmets with theirs. "Michael had a little difficulty, but he's fine. All our people from the J7-V are accounted for."

"Pass the word then. We'll follow Darkwood." Rourke told his friend.

"Right." And Paul was gone.

Darkwood seemed to be checking a compass, then touched helmets again. "If the German intelligence was correct, and we air-dropped pretty close to our target, like they say in the old western movies, 'thataway'!" And Darkwood gestured into the gloom below them and north.

"Thataway," John Rourke echoed.

The men of the team were already organizing themselves, using a wedge formation it appeared, standard Mid-Wake procedure. Two of the men swam ahead, as an advance guard, Rourke knew. Just as planned.

Darkwood's wings spread and he seemed to glide downward in an easy roll. Paul and Michael flanking him, John Rourke followed.

Chapter Twenty-eight

The water around him vibrated.

Jason Darkwood half furled his wings, hovering, feeling the shock wave build, strike, pass, the sensation like a gentle slap. The others would guess at what had happened, he knew, and there was no time for a conference. Just behind him, Dr. Rourke, Paul Rubenstein, and Michael Rourke waited, Sam Aldridge and the rest of the force behind them in a larger wedge, all hovering.

Darkwood unfurled his wings fully, gliding ahead through the water, using hands and flippers sparingly to conserve his strength, not fully recovered from his wounds but nearly so. The fatigue factor was something he had considered before deciding to volunteer, but again personal circumstances could not be helped. He was needed to do what had to be done.

Darkwood touched at his chest pack, shifting from vision intensification to magnification, always the wise choice first, lest one inadvertently focus in on something so bright that the intensified light was momentarily blinding. But, although there were shapes ahead, there was no bright light source. He added vision intensification to magnification.

And he saw the hull of a Soviet Island classer ahead, one of the more than three dozen missile-launching ports open but closing now as another two opened. Immediately, he switched off magnification and altered the beating of his wings, rolling, using both hands and flippers now as rapidly as he could.

Dr. Rourke, Michael, and Paul were close enough. Darkwood touched helmets with Rourke, the other two men touching helmets as well. "Tell everyone to make certain vision intensification is off. We have a launch imminent just ahead. I'll warn the advance guard. After the launch, join me."

"Right," Dr. Rourke said, wings beating faster now, swimming off immediately.

And Darkwood rolled again in the water, moving his wings as rapidly as possible now, propelling himself still faster through the water with hands and flippers.

His vision intensification was still on, but if it were not, he would be uncertain of finding the two advance guard personnel, at least one of them likely a German commando unused to the more subtle nuances of his equipment.

Darkwood skirted around a towering rock formation and through a school of cod, the creatures scattering about him.

Just ahead, he saw two figures. He changed direction to intercept them, touching at his chest pack to disengage vision intensification.

And the launch came, concussion hammering at him this time, a column of white vapor and churning water, the missile breaking surface as Darkwood was thrown back, into the rocks, his helmet slamming into an outcropping of coral, the water around him obscured in darkness as schools of fish abundant beyond credulity passed around him, over him, beneath him, their bodies crashing against his.

Automatically, he had furled his wings, and if he had not, Darkwood knew, they would have been destroyed.

His ears rang, his senses reverberating with the sounds from the launch. He braced himself, knowing the second launch was coming.

And come it did, Darkwood huddled in the rocks and coral now, creatures rising from the depth in their frantic rush to escape the source of their terror. As he tucked back deeper into his shelter, sailfish, horse-eye jacks, rays, and sharks passed him, thudding against him.

The ringing in Darkwood's ears persisted, but the concussion subsided. He pushed away from the rocks, dodging back as a large shark grazed past him.

Darkwood unfurled his wings, swimming toward the last position where he had seen the two advance guards.

He risked vision intensification again, scanning right to left, seeing one of the men, wings shredded, body twisted at an unnatural angle. Darkwood signaled down toward the man. A quick examination confirmed what logic had already suggested—dead. As quickly as he could now, before another launch, he began quartering to search for the second man.

Maria Leuden screamed and Annie grabbed the girl into her arms, dropping with her to her knees, just holding her as the mountain around them trembled and the platform on which they were sheltered gently swayed. Annie threw up the shawl that was around her shoulders, pulling it over her own head and Maria's as dust sprinkled down on them from the cavern ceiling above.

The low rumbling sound that had begun as barely a murmur, then grown, roaring, was subsiding now.

They were under attack.

Was it nuclear?

Annie Rubenstein told herself they'd be dead now if it had been.

Her husband, her brother, her father. Was it that they had not reached the Soviet submarines in time? Or . . .

But no pain cut through her, and she knew inside herself that if any of the three of them were to die, she would feel death as if she, too, were struck down. "Michael's fine, Maria! Take it easy," Annie reassured the girl who knelt, trembling, beside her. "We'll be safe here, too."

Safe, while above them the city itself might be in ruins, and soon Soviet surface forces would be attacking.

Annie looked along the platform. Her mother was beneath a table, on hands and knees. Natalia stood almost defiantly, the hood of her jacket raised, protecting her hair from the falling dust.

Annie hugged the girl closer. Maria whispered, "I wish there was something that we could do, but we cannot! It is terrible to be a woman."

Annie said nothing, holding the girl.

Her father had taught her, many years ago, and Paul's very existence confirmed, that life, was indeed, what you made it. Her eyes caught the eyes of her mother. They merely looked at one another across the dozens of women who sat or knelt about the platform, letting their fate rest in hands other than their own.

Her mother smiled.

Her mother nodded almost imperceptibly.

Annie held Maria tighter, because she wouldn't be holding the girl for long.

Chapter Twenty-nine

A body spiraled downward along the north wall of a narrow canyon about a thousand yards from the portside hull of the nearest Island Classer.

If the man were still alive—one of the Germans—he would surely die if he did not regain consciousness and slow or stop his descent.

As Darkwood hovered over the abyss, he felt a tap at the side of his helmet, thinking for a moment that a fish or something . . . It was Dr. Rourke. As their helmets touched, Rourke said, "You lost a man down there. Could he still be alive?"

"We lost a marine in the last detonation. That's a German in the canyon. If the German's alive, he won't be much longer. Keep the men sheltered while I go after him. After the next launch, approach the submarine, going for the stern. If I'm not back—"

"No. You're the only one who can pull off this mission. I'll go after him. You lead the men toward the submarine. I'll catch up. Remember, I've gone in through the aft airlock before. Plus, as a doctor, maybe I can do something for the man to save his life. Go on."

There wasn't time to argue, because each second took the hapless German to greater depth and brought the next missile firing that much closer. Darkwood said, "All right, Doctor, good luck," then clapped John Rourke on the shoulder. Rourke nodded almost imperceptibly, cocooning his wings around him as if he'd been diving with this equipment all his life, launching himself over the side of the canyon and into the abyss.

Darkwood watched after him for a split second more, then accelerated the beating of his wings, starting back toward the rest of the attack force. . . .

By using his flippers, arms locked against his sides, hands flat against his thighs except when he moved them slightly as stabilizers, John Rourke spiraled downward, keeping the pace of his descent within reason, but moving as rapidly as he could while still giving his suit the time to equalize pressure.

Below him, he could no longer see the man. Rourke touched at his chest pack, starting vision intensification again, well enough below the level of the nearest of the Soviet vessels that he felt he could risk it, even if firing were imminent.

Still no sign of the injured or unconscious—probably both—German commando.

Rourke activated magnification, following the heads-up navigational display in his helmet face plate to keep his orientation.

In the center of the face plate, where magnification had its effect, he saw a shape, odd-looking against a rock formation another sixty or seventy feet below him, but barely discernible despite magnification and vision intensification. Rourke slowed his descent still further.

He cocooned his wings, clinging to the rocky walls of the canyon, careful where he rested his hands despite the strength of his gloves. In these waters, there could be anything. There was a type of sea snake found in the Pacific—perhaps still found there, because deadly things had a habit of survival—whose bite always proved fatal, because the venom acted so quickly on the central nervous system that the victim expired in seconds, before any sort of medical procedure could even be begun.

John Rourke planned ahead. As he moved diagonally down the rock face, he reasoned that the next missile or missiles would launch soon and he had no idea what the shock wave might do in the confined space between the canyon walls. And so he clung to them.

And now the shock wave came, the noise of at least two

detonations rolling over him with it. Rourke's body was punched into the canyon wall, his hands barely able to still cling to the rock outcroppings.

Below him the dark shape moved, and Rourke realized it was, indeed, the man he sought. The man lay on the edge of an abyss even greater than the canyon, a trench of major proportions, running along the seafloor like a scar, toward the north and to the south.

Fish swarmed about Rourke, over him, around him as he held to his purchase against the canyon wall, large pieces of the very wall itself dislodging above and around him, rolling downward into the already churning waters surrounding him.

More rocks dislodged, a full-scale avalanche now. John Rourke pushed himself off from the canyon wall, no other choice now for his survival, letting his wings partly out, with his hands and his feet pulling him downward through the water and toward the German commando. The water moved with such violence, unexpected currents grabbing him, twisting him, that progress downward was slow. And as Rourke rolled through a spiral, above him he saw the upper portion of the rock wall shearing away in enormous sheets.

Rourke flexed and allowed the suit's wings to spread to full span. He kicked as powerfully as he could. To save the German and himself, he had to outdistance the rock falls or be pounded down into the depths of the trench, from which neither he nor the German commando would ever emerge alive.

The German was closer now, Rourke's arms going to maximum extension with each stroke, but the currents still so strong that for every foot of downward progress, he was pushed back at least half that distance, sometimes more. He glanced over his right shoulder, the rocks tumbling toward him in what seemed to be slow motion, like something out of a dream. If he merely cocooned his wings, letting the currents he fought draw him upward, chances were good that he'd survive.

But, as he gazed downward again, the German's body was about to slip over the edge.

John Rourke forced himself downward, grabbing at rock outcroppings, tugging himself past them for the last microsecond of speed.

There was another missile fired above him, but from farther away this time, another of the submarines from the Soviet armada opening fire on the German mountain city.

A sheet of rock slipped past him, twisting with the powerful currents, missing Rourke's left shoulder by inches.

There was no time to look above him. He shifted off magnification. Rourke kept swimming, pulling himself over a hummock of coral, reaching out his right hand and grabbing for the German commando as the man's body slipped over the edge and into the abyss. Rourke's right shoulder nearly dislocated under the sudden strain, his body twisting round as he fought to get a better grip on the man. And as Rourke's body orientation shifted, he saw a wall of rock crashing downward toward them, nearly on them.

There was no time to check the German's body to determine if the man were alive or dead. Rourke merely held to the body as tightly as he could and kicked off from the rock ledge and over into the abyss, cocooning his wings around him, letting the current seize them both.

Tons of rock crashed down onto the ledge, the ledge itself crumbling, all of it falling over into the abyss.

The current in which they were caught crossed through another, a whirlpool effect, Rourke's body and that of the German commando twisting in it, pummeled by its force. And then the second current had them, icy cold even through the dry suit, sucking them downward so rapidly there was no time to reach out and grab for something to hold on to, nothing to do but ride with it.

Their bodies spun in around the central vortex, nauseatingly quickly, dizziness grabbing at Rourke's consciousness now. And if he passed out, John Rourke knew, he would die here in this current, drawn even deeper into the abyss.

Chapter Thirty

Darkwood led the commandos forward, his eyes on the missile deck of the nearest Island Classer. If a missile were launched now, the shock wave would kill them.

And where was John Rourke? Had he been caught in the maelstrom of the multiple launches that had taken place seconds ago? If he had been, was he dead as logic suggested?

It was, somehow, impossible for Darkwood to imagine that, after all this time, these incredible perils that John Rourke had endured for more than five centuries, the man would be lost in an undersea tempest.

But there was no time left to think any further, because new hatches were opening on the missile deck of the nearest of the Island Classers, and any of the other ones—there were at least two more—might launch at any second. Exposed as they were, moving toward the Island Classer's stern, they would be killed. Once beneath her hull, however, they could take shelter there.

The fatigue was beginning to take its toll on Darkwood, and on one level of consciousness he was telling himself that he should not have come, as yet less than fully recovered from his wounds. But there had been no alternative. He kept swimming, no longer able to conserve physical energy and let wings alone propel him through the water, but forced by the necessity of time to actively swim, using hands as well as feet.

His eyes drifted to the Steinmetz on his wrist and he risked vision intensification to read it. There should be another launch in seconds.

Darkwood made a command decision, instructing the wedge of divers beginning on either side of him to veer off toward the underside of the Island Classer's hull. Precious time would be lost in reaching the hoped-for penetration point, but there was no choice if they were to survive.

And Darkwood swam now, toward the underside of the Island Classer's hull. . . .

John Rourke had nearly blacked out.

Thoughts of his children, of his wife, of Natalia came to him fleetingly, leaving just as quickly. Tired. If he closed his eyes . . . But John Rourke told himself, ordered himself, not to do that, because if he did, this time there would be no cheating death. The hemosponge would go on functioning almost infinitely. But the pressures at the depths to which the current would drag him would crush him.

And now, even with vision intensification on full, so little light penetrated within the abyss that Rourke could barely see the rock walls along which he sped. But on one level, deep within his consciousness, John Rourke's mind raced faster than his body. There had to be some way in which to stop this headlong lunge toward the depths of the abyss before he blacked out and was powerless.

And then a sudden realization struck John Rourke in the growing blackness as he clung to the body of a man who might well be dead and a current dragged him deeper into the abyss by the second: What if, this time, he did not survive?

Chapter Thirty-one

Annie Rourke Rubenstein screamed and clutched at her chest, her entire body gone limp. She fell forward, Maria Leuden beside her, screaming for help.

Inside herself, Annie saw, felt, infinite blackness, a wave of nausea passing over her, dizziness so intense that her consciousness began to ebb. "Natalia!"

"Momma!" The nausea again. "Nata—" Annie sprawled onto the floor of the platform, clutching at her throat, trying to hold back the blackness closing in around her.

"Annie?"

"Da—"

"Your father?"

"Da—Nata—" Walls of blackness closed around her and she was spinning, the blackness a blur going faster and faster. Her arms were no longer numb but ached from holding her body. But the body she held was not her own, and her mind was searching for something.

"Ann? What is it?"

"Mom—"

"Open the collar of her blouse, Natalia. She's having some sort of attack. I don't know—"

"There, Annie, try to breathe."

"We need a doctor! We need a doctor over here!"

The blackness deepened and welled up within her mind, blotting out thought now. Her arms hurt so badly, and she wanted to reach out to something and stop. Above her, she saw her mother's face, Natalia's face. She heard Maria screaming for help.

Hands touched at her.

She couldn't let go of the body she held so tightly. The darkness was consuming her. . . .

142

John Rourke's arms ached.

And he was aware of the body that he held more than he had been an instant earlier. Why? This guy was going to die, too? Was that it?

The heel of Rourke's right hand rested against something hard. What was it?

Only a very small portion of his mind still functioned, like a tiny white dot surrounded by encroaching blackness, nearly blotted out. What could this object be? He searched and searched and wondered if perhaps the information he sought were not within the boundaries of that ever-shrinking white dot.

But, at last, he found what he sought.

The object was an explosive charge for use against the screw of an Island Classer, in the event the vessel could not be penetrated but had to be crippled instead. Several members of each team from the J7-Vs carried these charges with them, for use against the main screws and other vulnerable areas of the monstrous-sized submarines.

John Rourke felt a momentary glow of pride. He had remembered.

The white dot was closing in, and for some reason he knew now that he had to push back the blackness surrounding it, and if he could accomplish that, the other thing that had started nagging at him would be recognizable, retrievable from his mind.

What was that?

Something about the explosive charge.

And the nature of a current.

As he spun uncontrollably and inside himself fought back the blackness, he tried to remember what it was that he was supposed to remember. . . .

Several missiles fired as if in battery, Jason Darkwood felt it was at least marginally safe to proceed. He signaled Michael Rourke and Paul Rubenstein aft with half the remaining men along the portside of the submarine's underbelly, Sam Aldridge and the balance of the men accompanying Darkwood to starboard.

Darkwood's eyes focused on the dual display of his Steinmetz. In three minutes, the agreed-upon time would be reached, and if the submarine could be breached, it would.

German Intelligence overflights had hinted strongly at three Soviet vessels positioned offshore, and going on that assumption Dr. Rourke had elected targets for each of the teams air-dropped from the J7-Vs designating the Island Classers simply as numbers one through three, number one being the vessel farthest south, number three the vessel farthest north.

And each team was given a predesignated rendezvous time and location.

Two minutes and forty-three seconds remained until the three teams designated to assault Island Classer number one, Darkwood's one of the three, were to rendezvous beneath the main diver access hatch.

And where was John Rourke?

Darkwood, a Soviet Sty-20 pneumatic in his right fist, his helmet on vision intensification, swam ahead.

If a single flipper tip touched prematurely against the Island Classer's hull, the mission would be blown. If a random video scan caught them, and the operator were observant or the scan were computer linked, they would be equally undone. Fish, of course, would graze against the side of a submarine on station keeping speed, essentially hovering in the water in neutral buoyancy. But each such touch meant an automatic video scan of the hull. And the hulls of Island Classers, like something out of Jules Verne, could be electrified. Any living creature touching the hull would meet instant death.

If intruders were detected—of the human kind—there were various standard options within the Soviet Navy, the most potentially deadly among them the release of what American naval personnel had dubbed Claymore Clusters, clusterlike charges similar to those used defensively in the United States Navy by attack submarines like the *Reagan*, of which Darkwood was captain. But, unlike standard cluster charges, which were high explosive, these antipersonnel cluster charges employed by the Soviet Fleet were similar in nature to the Claymore Mines of the Vietnam War more than five centuries ago.

When the Claymore Clusters were triggered, a comparatively small explosive charge propelled thousands of nearly microscopic fiberglass darts in all directions. The darts were not strong enough to penetrate or even stick to the hull of the Island Classer from which they originated, but were amply strong to penetrate the suit of a diver.

Darkwood had seen men — twice — who had fallen victim to Claymore Clusters. Very little recognizable as human had remained of them.

He swam on. . . .

John Rourke's little white spot was merely a spec now, and thoughts of his wife and daughter and son and Paul and Natalia — the only people in his adult life that he had ever loved — seemed much more important to him now than trying to recall what it was he could do with the explosive charge the German commando had secured to his utility belt.

And, even if somehow he were able to stop the flow of the current, how could he ever find his way back to the rest of the attack force going against the Island Classers? Time eluded him completely now, and minutes or hours or anything between might have passed since he'd fallen victim to the current.

Indeed, Rourke smiled within his helmet, stopping the flow of the current would be as likely as stopping the flow of time itself.

And his arms were weary of holding the German, but he would not let go while the will to try to save the man was still with him.

He would hang on.

And, soon, the darkness would eradicate even that one tiny white speck remaining to him.

Chapter Thirty-two

Sarah Rourke held her daughter's head against her breast. Annie whispered, not as the needle—Sarah had inquired and it was an injection of a mild sedative—had punctured her arm, but afterward, as the sedative began to take its effect. "He's dying—dying—Daddy!? He—"

"Jesus," Sarah whispered, her lips touching at Annie's hair, her hands caressing her daughter's face. Annie was experiencing her father's death. John.

Without him, what would there be?

Sarah shivered.

Natalia's voice beside Sarah Rourke was calmer than she ever would have expected it to be. "He's more than mortal. How can he die?"

And Natalia began to cry.

Sarah Rourke's left arm moved toward Natalia as the woman dropped to her knees beside them. Her arm folded around Natalia and she drew her head to her shoulder, holding her.

Annie's voice, strange, detached, came again. "One little spot."

Annie's gift of the mind, as Sarah Rourke had always thought it to be, was the most horrible of curses. Annie was, mentally, experiencing her father's death as surely as if somehow she were inside him, as if she were her father.

And Sarah Rourke wondered, when the actual moment came, would Annie die, too?

Natalia cried. Sarah kissed Natalia's forehead. "We're in this together, all of us; and nothing will change that."

Natalia started to pull away.

Sarah held her. "You don't have to be strong now."

And Natalia's arms went around Sarah, her body heaving

with heavy sobs.

Annie whispered, ". . . stopping the flow . . . stopping the flow . . . the . . ."

Sarah Rourke held her daughter and her rival, held them as tightly as she could.

And tears filled her eyes.

The platform shook. Another missile had struck. Dust from the cavern ceiling streamed down on them, Sarah averting her eyes. Perhaps Annie's curse was a blessing in disguise. Because if the missiles successfully destroyed the mountain and the cavern ceiling were to collapse on them, Annie might be so consumed by her father's death that she would be spared the experience of her own.

Sarah bit her lower lip, holding on to these two women, both of them closer to her than any sisters could ever have been. And as she looked away for a moment, she saw Maria Leuden, hands cupped in front of her, eyes downcast, for all the world looking like some woebegone little girl who had done some terrible thing and now expected to be punished.

Sarah tried to speak. She couldn't. She cleared her throat. "Maria, come kneel beside me."

And Maria Leuden, haltingly, hesitantly, came forward, dropping to her knees. Sarah's right hand reached out to Maria, taking the girl's hand and holding it tightly.

". . . the flow."

Chapter Thirty-three

John Rourke's little white dot began to close over, but as it did, the flow of blackness was halted. ". . . the flow."

The explosive charge.

John Rourke fought against the blackness. ". . . the flow."

If he could stop the flow of time . . . no. Time wasn't what he needed to stop. The current.

If he could stop the flow of the current . . .

The white dot began to grow, pushing back the blackness. At the edge of the white dot, there had to be a portion of clinical reasoning remaining, because he realized that it was a new adrenaline rush pushing back the blackness.

But the adrenaline wouldn't last that long.

The explosive charge. The flow.

The walls of the abyss shot past him. No. That wasn't right. They were massive sheets of rock, stationary. He was moving past them, spiraling round and round and round. The blackness was closing in again. He fought it back.

Use the charge.

Activate the timer.

Set the charge.

Stop the flow.

Time?

No. Stop the flow of the current.

The walls of rock.

John Rourke began flexing the fingers of his right hand, moving them down the German commando's ribcage and to the explosive charge attached to the man's utility belt. . . .

They touched helmets, Jason Darkwood, Sam Aldridge, and the commander of the second team. They hovered beneath the primary hatch. Sam Aldridge said, "I should do it. You're beat already, Jase."

"Captain Jase, Sam, hmm? No. You guys wait, I'll lock the missile hatch."

"And what if you don't swim fast enough, Captain? You're dead, then, and you're the only one of us qualified to take command of this friggin' Island Classer once we're inside."

"I swim fast enough, Sam." And Darkwood holstered the Sty-20, then took the bar that was taped alongside Sam Aldridge's right thigh. Sam was right, of course, but as they'd swum their way aft, Darkwood had come to the realization that John Rourke was likely dead and wouldn't have been if he hadn't let the doctor talk him out of the dangerous thing, just so he could get inside the Island Classer.

He wouldn't cost another man his life this day if he could help it.

Sam Aldridge was holding onto the bar. "Let it go, Sam. That's an order."

His life-long friend let go of the bar. "You get killed, I'm pissed, Jase."

"Well, we wouldn't want you ticked off, would we, Sam?" And Aldridge pulled back from the huddle, let his wings flex, and rolled, then started swimming up along the submarine's starboard side hull and toward the missile deck. . . .

John Rourke's right hand fumbled for the timer control on the explosive charge. If he took the charge from the German commando's belt, he wouldn't have enough hands to get the job done. The white dot was larger now, holding its own, but with difficulty.

The charges had been preset for two minutes, but the diode timers could be changed. He desperately wanted to lower that time now, but there was no way to see what he might be doing to the timer until he removed the charge from the utility belt. And he would have a second or less to attach it before the current swept it from him. Not enough time to even begin to alter the timer.

He found the control that activated the timer.

He memorized its position.

Now Rourke's hand moved from the charge to the belt, determining how best to release the charge from the utility belt. The Germans used a modified version of the Bianchi clip, which had replaced the Alice clip in the days before The Night of The War. Rourke's fingers found the rolled ends of the clip, freeing one of them so the clip was only half secured to the belt.

Now his fingers moved back along the shape of the charge to the rear of it, where the timer interlock was positioned. He activated the switches in sequence, his fingers almost too thick for the controls.

He flipped the last switch.

Two minutes.

Was there room inside the white dot to count seconds?

He abandoned the idea, because if the plan worked, he might just live. If it didn't, he would surely die.

His hand moved toward the clip, his fingers prying at the second rolled piece. It didn't want to budge. John Rourke almost laughed.

Now at least he knew how he would die. He would blow himself up and take the German commando with him.

"Damnit," Rourke rasped into his helmet.

His own voice sounded very odd to him, tired but familiar. . . . His gloved fingers tore at the clip and he popped it loose, the charge nearly torn from his grasp as he grabbed for it.

But he had it.

Spiraling.

Where was the wall?

Now was a good time to think about that, he told himself.

Grasping the charge as tightly as he could, John Rourke pushed it away from his body, forcing his eyes to focus in the almost total blackness surrounding him. Was that a crack or a shadow?

It was gone.

He forced himself to watch more carefully.

How many seconds remained?

150

He had no idea.

He laughed. "Do or die!"

A crack, nice and wide.

John Rourke punched the charge into the crack, his right hand nearly torn away, part of the outer layer of the glove ripped away, he guessed.

How many seconds?

Together, both arms wrapped around the body of the man, they spun downward, deeper and deeper.

And behind John Rourke, there was a roar.

And the roar grew and grew, Rourke's body and the body of the German slamming against the wall of the abyss. They stopped. Nausea swept over him.

The current.

". . . the flow."

A wall of rock tumbled toward them, blocking the flow of the current as it was sidetracked around. But John Rourke knew on the most primitive level of intelligence that if he stayed where he was, the rock would crush him, and if it did not, then the current would grab them again.

Rourke held the German in his left arm and reached out with his right, praying that his wings still functioned. He flung himself and the German commando away from the wall and into the black water beyond, tons of rock crashing around them, the already nearly nonexistent light further obscured as loose dirt and debris dislodged by the avalanche formed a cloud around them. A current eddied across the void, Rourke twisting his body to escape it, dragging the German with him.

The water churned around them.

Rourke held the German commando to him.

And as the last of the rocks tumbled away into the deeper reaches of the abyss, Rourke hovered there in the water with the German still in his arms.

And there was nothing but silence and darkness.

Chapter Thirty-four

Annie had fallen quiet, and Sarah assumed the sedative had taken its full effect.

Maria Leuden held Annie's hand as she knelt beside her.

The bombardment continued, Natalia's hair and the shoulders of her black jumpsuit streaked grey with dust. Sarah shook her own hair carefully, dust falling from it onto her BDU blouse and black pants. Natalia had stopped crying now, and she knelt back on her heels and began to speak calmly. "If he dies, even if we win, I cannot help but feel all of this was for nothing."

"No. Don't say that. Look at you."

Natalia almost laughed. "I am covered with dust. I'm trapped where my only real skills are valueless. Look at me, indeed."

"No," Sarah insisted. "Look at who you were and who you are, what you've survived and triumphed over. You were on the wrong side, but instead of a devil, you were only a slightly tarnished angel. And John helped you to realize that. You even went through a nervous breakdown and survived that . . . triumphed. You're a better person today than you ever were."

Natalia did smile this time. "Isn't it odd, you and I being friends?"

Sarah looked down at her abdomen, smiling. "Yes. We both love the same man. I guess that gives us a lot in common. And I'm glad you're my friend. And despite things, I think we always would have remained friends."

"I'll stay with you and the others until your baby's come, if you like. You're pretty good at protecting yourself, but for a while you might need a protector."

"A friend," Sarah corrected. "And I'll need a friend always."

"Look!"

It was Maria who spoke and Sarah turned toward the girl, who was staring at Annie. There was a look of peacefulness on the face of her daughter, which Sarah Rourke had not seen before.

"Do you think—" Natalia began, her voice catching.

"Yes. Maybe. He's hard to kill, the man we love." And Sarah Rourke took Natalia's right hand and squeezed it tightly. . . .

Jason Darkwood hovered by the rail of the Island Classer's missile deck, vision intensification off but the missile hatches close enough that he could see them clearly at the depth. The filtered sunlight overhead and the face of his wristwatch agreed. Mid-morning now, nearly as bright as it would get at the depth. Mid-Wake Naval Intelligence knew very little about the Island Class submarines' missile launching procedures, but Sebastian, first officer of the *Reagan,* was one of the two smartest men Jason Darkwood knew. John Rourke, likely dead now, was the second. And Sebastian had calculated a computer program on the launch sequence system of the Soviet Island Classers' missiles. As Darkwood surveyed the missile deck now, matching closed by contrail-blackened hatch areas, Sebastian's program seemed to be holding.

"It is relatively simple, Jason, to a point. Admiral Severinski's chief of staff, as we well know, is a devotee of chess and piano, both devotions much to his credit, may I add. In chess, of course, there are thirty-two pieces, sixteen major and sixteen pawns."

"Yes, Sebastian, thirty-two pieces. So what?"

"There are forty missile tubes, Jason." And Sebastian had cocked his eyebrows, Darkwood getting the distinct impression that his tall, lean, muscular, and extraordinarily intelligent black first officer expected him—Jason Darkwood—to draw some marvelous conclusion from the relationship between the numbers thirty-two and forty. Darkwood took a stab at it. "The missile deck incorporates one-fifth more

153

tubes than the number of men on the chessboard."

"Actually, the chessboard incorporates four fifths of the number of missile tubes, Jason, but indeed, fifths are the key."

"Fifths? You mean, like fifths of whiskey?

Sebastian had smiled, not indulgently (thank God), but as if sharing Darkwood's joke, which hadn't been intended as a joke at all. "Yes . . . well, the Soviet Fleet Grade officers have been known to imbibe a bit, I suppose, although vodka is their usual preference. But I refer, of course, to the interval of five diatonic degrees, or the tones of the standard major and minor scale to the exclusion of the chromatics. So, if the forty missile tubes were viewed as forty keys on the piano, where, of course, there would normally be eighty-eight, then we proceed from the point of origin by whole steps. Therefore, whichever missile tube were fired first would serve as the starting note, but would, of necessity, be a whole step. Further, assuming the progression would begin to approximate Middle C, which would most closely approximate the number of tubes as opposed to the number of keys remaining on the piano, then the missiles would fire in sequence of the sixth, the thirteenth, the eighteenth, and so on. Once that progression is exhausted, I confess to being totally befuddled. The program within the computer of the Roy Rogers" — the name given the captured Island Classer Sebastian currently commanded — "is so deeply encoded as to be currently indecipherable. So, dependent on whether the reference point were fore or aft, the sequence would involve firing the sixth, then the thirteenth, then the eighteenth tube, moving on to the twenty-fifth and then the thirtieth, etc. Once the firing possibilities were exhausted, unless the program were devised by someone who wished his logic to be almost diabolically obtuse, one might readily assume that the progression would be begun again, run until the battery were fully exhausted, but this latter is, I'm afraid, mere supposition, Jason."

"Oh."

Jason Darkwood eyed what should, following Sebastian's mathematical progression, be the next tube fired. If it fired

154

as he approached, he was dead. If, after he accomplished his bit of sabotage, the tube were still fired, they'd all be dead, because the submarine itself would explode. If a second tube were fired, simultaneously with the first, the result might be either his death alone or the destruction of the submarine, hence the death of all of them.

"Fraught with peril," Jason Darkwood muttered into his helmet.

And he swam forward, with the precisely turned crowbar-shaped rod in his right fist.

He crossed over the missile deck, careful lest a flipper inadvertently touch against its surface, his eyes riveted to the next tube Sebastian's reasoning suggested would fire. There was no movement of the hatch, nothing but Sebastian's second-guessing the Soviet computer programmer to make Darkwood select this very hatch.

And, at last, he hovered over it. Carefully, he let himself down over the hatch, hoping the hatch lid was not sensitized, hoping, too, that video observation would not detect his presence.

He bent over the hatch and inserted the rod between the double hinges, effectively—he hoped—locking the hatch in the closed position.

As his hands moved away from the rod, the hatch moved, started upward, Darkwood swimming away, using wings, flippers, and hands. As he glanced back, the tube hatch had reached a height of approximately two inches off level from the deck. And it raised no farther. Darkwood quickened his pace, because the first reaction of the launch crew would be to get a visual fix on the nature of the problem.

And, with any luck at all, once it was realized the hatch was jammed, a frogman team would be dispatched to manually open it.

And they would come through the main diver lock near which his attack force waited—with any luck.

Chapter Thirty-five

John Rourke pushed the body of the German commando into a natural cavelike niche in the wall of the abyss. There was finally time now to check the man, to see if he were alive or dead.

Free from the overwhelmingly powerful current that had driven them downward, John Rourke realized there was no time for any other consideration but to escape the current before it could reclaim them. The chances of two such powerful currents — essentially underwater rivers — being so terribly close to one another within the walls of the abyss into which they'd been pulled were exceedingly remote. Yet, they would never escape this current or a similar one if captured again, so any chance was too great a risk.

He judged they had traveled upward for more than a hundred feet before finding the little cave. Inside it now, Rourke first examined the German to determine whether or not the man still lived, which, indeed, he did.

Exhaustion and relief tempted John Rourke to lean back against the cave wall and rest, but because the German was alive now didn't mean the man would survive. Carefully, Rourke began the difficult task of examining the unconscious but regularly breathing German commando through the dry suit. He found evidence to suggest that the man had suffered several cracked ribs, but none of them seemed broken; and, as best Rourke could ascertain under the circumstances, neither lung seemed punctured. His initial examination for obvious head or back or neck injuries complete, Rourke began to examine the man in greater detail. His eyes were closed, and there was no way to check pupillary reaction without compromising the protection of the dry suit and killing the man. His breathing was still regular, but in the beam of

Rourke's flashlight the man's color seemed pale, even for a blond-haired German.

Shock, obviously, but the suit would aid in keeping the man supplied with breathable air and warm at the same time; and, evidently, Rourke's own manipulation of the body while holding on to the man had aided in keeping him respirating.

The important thing was to get the man to the surface, where proper medical treatment could be administered—to the surface or into a submarine.

John Rourke felt a smile cross his lips.

He worked the chest pack, punching up coordinates and trying to determine his position in relationship to the Soviet Island Classers above.

As best he could tell, he was a mile away from the original Island Classer and another hundred feet below it. How far he and the German had traveled while stuck in the current was impossible to determine, because his heads-up readout indicated more than seven miles traversed. It seemed impossible to consider that the current had wound so intricately within the abyss.

In any event, Rourke decided, the best option was to go straight up, reassess his position, then try to rejoin Darkwood and the rest of the attack force. By now, they might well have penetrated the Soviet vessel. But if they had, why were there missiles still firing?

Like distant claps of spring thunder, John Rourke could hear them.

He checked his and the German's suits, then eased the man into his arms, like an adult would carry a child. Using wings and flippers alone, Rourke launched them from the lip of the cave mouth and into open water again, starting upward. . . .

They sheltered in the coral and rocks about fifty yards off the Island Classer's main diver lock, just aft of the Island Classer's towering sail.

When the second and third Island Classer—Darkwood

was reasonably certain there were only two more — had fired their missiles, another storm of violent currents, rock particles, and silt had washed toward them in a fast-moving wave. But they survived, and now, with the hatch opening, missile firings from the other two vessels would logically be halted while friendly divers were in the water.

There was a broad shaft of yellow light, piercingly strong, and the hatch was fully open. The Soviet divers began exiting in order to repair the hatch over the missile tube, security with the rifle versions of Sty-20 shark guns guarding the hatchway.

Jason Darkwood and the men clustered around him on the rock shelf waited.

At least, the bombardment of the German mountain city was temporarily ended.

How much devastation the missile strikes might have wrought was anyone's guess, and clearly, even given his limited experience in surface warfare, the missile attack was merely the softening up prior to a full-scale assault.

There were literally thousands of Soviet personnel in the field, their armor obviously superior, their air power virtually a match for the German air power from everything Jason Darkwood had heard.

The only significant German advantage — aside from right being on their side, which as an American, Darkwood had always taken as a definite plus — was that the Germans fought from a strongly defended home base, with easily accessed lines of supply.

If that advantage were to be neutralized, right being on the side of the Allied cause or not, the Germans stood an excellent chance of being defeated.

And Darkwood's only possibility of being able to reverse that potential for disaster was a hatch opening about six feet wide, some fifty yards away.

He waited. . . .

At the height of the abyss, John Rourke lay down his burden — the German commando — and once again worked with the elements of his chest pack to reassess his position based on the heads-up display within his helmet visor. A mile or a little better from at least one of the Island Classers, which one being another question entirely.

So, again, John Rourke took up his injured comrade. He shook his head as a silly thought crossed his mind. He remembered the pop song of the 1960s. If only the German had been his brother, at least according to the song's lyrics, he wouldn't have been heavy.

Using wings and flippers only, John Rourke swam on.

Chapter Thirty-six

Annie rested comfortably. Natalia at last left her side, telling herself that John had to be alive, that the peaceful, almost joyous look on Annie's face in repose meant just that.

In the restroom facility, she brushed as much of the dust from her hair as she could, waited for an empty stall—it seemed like half the women there had to use the bathroom at the same time—and did what was necessary. She rezipped her jumpsuit, took her gunbelt and shoulder holster from the hook on the inside of the door, and redonned them. She left the stall, returned to the mirror, ran a brush through her hair again for good measure, then took one of the black silk bandannas from her purse. She tied it over her head, knotting it under her hair at the nape of the neck.

"Babushka," she smiled, taking a last look at herself in the mirror, then walking out.

Annie would have been a valuable ally in this, but she would be sedated for another several hours.

The bombardment had stopped, which meant one of three possibilities was the likely scenario. Either John's commando force had succeeded, the city had already fallen, or the bombardment had merely been suspended to allow elements of the Soviet land force to attack.

In either of the last two scenarios, being trapped in this underground vault meant certain death or capture. But, outside of it, there were possibilities. One determined person could make a difference with the necessary skills to back up that determination. Other persons could be found, resistance offered.

In any event, here she was useless.

She walked past Sarah and Maria, the former mouthing a silent "Good luck" and the latter smiling. Annie rested between them on an inflatable mattress.

Some of the other women in safe storage here looked at her oddly as she moved past them, some whispering, some smiling, some casting looks of disapproval.

Many women considered it unfeminine to go about in sturdy high boots and black battle dress and openly quite heavily armed. But Natalia Anastasia Tiemerovna had never considered doing the right thing unfeminine. Let them watch her, let them remark that she was being a fool or forgetting her place — whatever that was — or anything they liked.

Natalia approached two of the female German officers standing off some distance from the female enlisted guards in the vaultlike doorway that sealed the Leader Bunker in which they waited.

As she approached the officers — both lieutenants — they came to attention, the evident senior of the two addressing her as "Fräulein Major!"

"Lieutenant, I wish to leave the Leader Bunker to go to aid in the fighting in the city above us."

The woman looked nonplussed. "But, Fräulein Major, it is impossible to —"

Natalia shrugged her shoulders, her right palm opening, a click-click-click sound and the Bali-Song exposed, the tip of the Wee-Hawk blade at the woman's throat. "Have the door opened now, and I wish an assault rifle and twelve loaded magazines. After I have passed through, you will secure the entry, allowing no one to pass in or out except as relates to your existing orders. Any attempt to stop me and you" — Natalia looked the woman straight in her startled corn-flower-blue eyes — "die. If you know my reputation, then you know I do not indulge in idle threats, Lieutenant."

"But —" Natalia let the point of the Bali-Song touch the skin of the woman's throat, not enough to puncture, but just enough to be felt. "Yes, Fräulein Major!"

"You," Natalia told one of the door guards, "hurry with the assault rifle!"

Chapter Thirty-seven

Inside the elevator, she checked the assault rifle, the action smooth enough and the firing pin in place, everything as it should be. Periodically, squatted on the floor as she inspected the rifle, she looked at the female German officer whom she had brought along as elevator operator, insurance against getting the power cut off from below, stranding her.

Natalia had the woman on her knees in the opposite corner, hands behind her head, face into the corner, like some bad child being punished in school.

"Fräulein Major?"

"Do not talk, Lieutenant. This is a short enough ride, and then you can resume your duties."

"But, you cannot—I would like to fight as well, but there are orders, Fräulein Major."

"I am not in your army, Lieutenant. And there are imperatives higher than any orders." Natalia was satisfied that the rifle was acceptable to her needs. She inserted a forty-round magazine up the well, a second forty-round magazine of caseless ammunition clipped to the first. As Natalia started to her feet, the German officer wheeled and threw herself across the elevator cabin, tackling her. Natalia's body slammed against the wall, her breath lost for a second. The German lieutenant's right knee smashed upward as her left hand slapped outward. Natalia pivoted slightly right, taking the knee smash in the fleshy portion of her left hip. But the slap caught her, and Natalia's head snapped back with its force.

The German's right fist punched into her abdomen, Natalia starting to double over with it but bringing her right hand from above her head downward quickly, backhanding the woman across the right cheek with her knuckles.

162

As Natalia sank to her knees, the German lieutenant fell back.

But the German woman was quick. She pushed away from the wall, throwing herself toward Natalia.

Natalia let herself fall the rest of the way forward and left, rolling, her left foot snapping out as she took her weight on her right hip, her foot catching the German officer in the rib cage just under the right breast.

The German sucked in her breath in something like a scream, but not loud enough. She was up again as Natalia rolled to her feet and she charged, both hands going for Natalia's throat and face, her nails like claws.

The principal reason why many women did not adapt well to hand-to-hand combat was that so many of them fought instinctively like women — scratch and claw and gouge and tear and twist and pinch.

Natalia did not fight that way, although she could when the situation called for it.

She wheeled right into a three hundred sixty degree pirouettelike turn on her left foot, her right back-kicking at the German. But the German was quicker than Natalia judged her to be, and Natalia's foot caught the woman on the right shoulder instead of the right side of the head as the woman dodged back. But there was not sufficient force in the kick to break her collarbone or dislocate her shoulder, because Natalia had no desire to kill an ally who was just trying to do her duty as she saw it.

The woman rocked back.

Natalia feigned another flying kick as the woman charged again, but she halted in mid move, letting the German officer dodge the kick. As the lieutenant moved to block the kick that wasn't coming, Natalia's balled left fist hooked upward and right, catching her on the right side of the jaw and knocking her down. Natalia threw herself onto the woman, the heel of her right hand impacting the German officer just below the left ear, knocking her out.

"Sorry," Natalia almost whispered, looking up from the floor to the elevator level indicator. Nearly there. Natalia got

163

to her feet, retying the bandanna, which had fallen round her neck, under her hair. She grabbed up the assault rifle, the magazine carrier, and her black bag, then racked the bolt of the rifle.

The elevator stopped.

The doors opened.

Natalia ran, twisting the key for the level of the Leader Bunker, slipping between the doors an instant before they thwacked shut.

She was in the sub-basement of the National Defense Headquarters.

And she stopped.

Around her, there was nothing but silence.

Natalia Anastasia Tiemerovna let her rifle fall to her side on its sling, took her black gloves from her bag—the knuckles of her left fist hurt a little—and pulled them on.

She eschewed any more elevators, running for the stairs.

Chapter Thirty-eight

The swimmers were returning to the airlock hatch.

With hand and arm movements, Jason Darkwood signaled the others to be ready. Michael Rourke, Paul Rubenstein, and Sam Aldridge crouched beside him.

Darkwood tapped Sam Aldridge and Michael Rourke on the shoulder and at the far right edge of his peripheral vision he saw young Rourke pass the signal on to Paul Rubenstein. Then the four of them were moving, fanning out from cover, swimming as fast as they could toward the airlock, the divers — except for the security personnel — already entering, most having nearly disappeared inside.

In Darkwood's right hand he held the identical duplicate of the Randall Smithsonian Bowie his ancestor Nathaniel Darkwood had brought with him to Mid-Wake five centuries ago. He glanced at Aldridge first, then at young Rourke, then at Rubenstein. Aldridge carried his copy of the Ka-Bar United States Marine Corps Knife, Rourke the Crain Life Support System I made for him at Lydveldid Island by a swordmaker known as Old Jon, after the design of the Crain knife from five centuries ago. Rubenstein's knife was the only genuine antique, a five-century-old spear-pointed Gerber Mk II fighting knife, a design conceived during the Vietnam War.

They moved on the shark-gun-armed security team.

There were seven of them, and the two nearest Darkwood, Rourke, Rubenstein, and Aldridge turned suddenly, as if somehow — even though it was impossible — they had heard something. As one of the Soviet security team personnel raised his shark gun to fire, Paul Rubenstein's body slammed against him. Sea Wings cocooned around Rubenstein's body, his knife powering forward into the Soviet Marine Spetznas's throat. The water around them was clouded dark with blood.

Darkwood was nearest the second of the two already-alerted men, his left arm moving to block the shark gun, his right arm pistoning into the Soviet's chest.

As Darkwood drew out the knife, Aldridge was already locked in combat with two of the Marine Spetznas, Michael Rourke finishing another of them with a swipe of his fighting knife across the man's throat. Darkwood moved toward the hatchway, the airlock door closing as the remaining two Marine Spetznas guards moved to seal it.

Darkwood raked his knife across the lower back of one of them, hoping to catch the spine, a cloud of blood obscuring his vision. The second of the two men stroked upward with the butt of his gun, Darkwood twisting away from it, losing his balance, rolling over and right.

As the Marine Spetznas turned his gun around to fire, Darkwood let the Randall fall from his right hand and made ready to draw the Sty-20 from his hip, knowing the man wouldn't make it.

The security man's body seemed to freeze, and then his arms snapped away from his body.

As the body floated forward, Jason Darkwood saw a tall figure, Sea Wings cocooned around his shoulders, a gleaming knife with an impossibly long blade in his right hand, a smaller cloud of blood than that from the dead Marine Spetznas floating around the knife's blade.

It was Dr. Rourke.

Chapter Thirty-nine

John Rourke rolled left through the water, flexing his shoulders to use the Sea Wings for balance, drawing them tight around him as, hands and flippers, he propelled himself toward the hatchway.

A gloved hand was reaching over the lip of the hatch, pushing it downward to close, and John Rourke hacked upward and outward with the LS-X, chopping the hand off.

Reflexively, regardless of the protection provided by his helmet and visor, Rourke averted his eyes from the blood spray. His left hand reached down to twist free the shark gun still in the grip of one of the dead Marine Spetznas personnel as his right hand sheathed the knife. Rourke fired the shark gun up through the hatchway, hoping to find a target, then rammed the gun between the hatch and the flange, wedging it there as he pushed himself through and came up into the spout rising out of the center of the open hatch. Grab rings above him, Rourke reached up for them. A Marine Spetznas lunged toward him with an issue Soviet knife, Rourke's hands clinging to the rings as he pulled himself up and swung, both feet impacting the man in the chest, knocking him reeling away.

Rourke was out of the spout, and he jumped clear of the hatch. As the Marine Spetznas brought up his knife, Rourke kicked him in the head, knocking the man senseless against the bulkhead.

Two Marine Spetznas in full diving gear raised shark guns to fire, Rourke drawing his knife with his left hand, hacking outward with it in a long arc, severing the brachial artery of one of the men. Already, Rourke's right hand moved to free the Sty-20 from the holster along his right thigh, the holster's release system complicated and slow. The other Marine Spetznas fired and Rourke dodged right.

167

The shark spear ricocheted off the flange. Rourke's right hand had the Sty-20 from its holster at last, and he stabbed the dart gun upward and right, firing, impaling the Marine Spetznas with a dart into the abdomen just beneath the sternum. Rourke fired again, hitting the man in the throat.

Two more Marine Spetznas jumped from the secondary hatchway above, Rourke backstepping, firing the Sty-20 three times into the right cheek of the helmetless man nearest him. The second of them body-slammed against John Rourke, the Sty-20 falling from Rourke's grasp and clattering to the floor. As Rourke and the Marine Spetznas impacted the bulkhead, Rourke's right knee smashed up, his left fist — still holding the knife — crashing across the man's jaw, the butt of the knife like a yarawa stick or a roll of quarters from five centuries ago.

The Soviet's head snapped back, Rourke's right fist pistoning upward, catching him full beneath the jaw, driving the man back. Rourke hacked outward with the Crain LS-X and tore open the man's throat.

He was inside and John Rourke was suffocating, the hemosponge useless in atmosphere. Rourke tore off his helmet, lightheaded at the sudden change in pressure and air quality.

The interior airlock door. Rourke ran toward the ladder, grabbing up another of the shark guns from a dead Marine Spetznas. He kicked out of his flippers, scaling the ladder as quickly as he could, then bracing the shark gun against the operating wheel so it could not be turned until he wished it so.

Grabbing onto a vertical, the Crain LS-X in his left hand, Rourke swung down back to the level of the outer lock.

Water spouted there in a heavy white stream more than two feet high now, the force of the sea around them being held back by air pressure alone.

A figure was breaking through the water spout and John Rourke leveled the Sty-20 toward it, but he recognized the suit markings as Mid-Wake in origin. The man grabbed onto the ring grips above and swung out of the spout, Rourke lowering the muzzle of the Sty-20.

The figure removed the helmet, which obscured his face. The face was Jason Darkwood's.

"You all right, Doctor? I thought—"

"I thought I was, too, Jason. Come on!" More of the Mid-Wake personnel were coming up through the hatchway, Paul and Michael leading them. "Michael! Airlock!"

"Right!" And Michael began shouting orders as Paul moved to the controls for the outer lock, two of the other men aiding him, closing it manually as the unconscious German whose life Rourke had saved was pushed through, Sam Aldridge following him. The lock was sealed. "They'll kill pressure in here! Hurry!" Michael shouted to the three men helping him.

"Hatch secure!" Paul sang out.

Sam Aldridge barked orders to the rest of the commando team, "Be ready to give 'em something they don't expect once that interior hatch is blown! Look sharp!"

John Rourke looked to the hatch above, the rope of what was the German equivalent of plastic nearly out of the waterproof tube in which it was packed. Darkwood assisted Michael in setting the detonator, others erecting the blast shield. "Hurry with that!" John Rourke ordered, physically assisting in mating the pieces together.

"Almost ready, Dad!" Michael called.

Paul was beside John Rourke now, aiding in assembling the roof panels. The end result looked like an igloo without a doorway, domed to deflect both shock wave and debris, constructed of a petroleum-based metalized plastic material that was both fireproof and bulletproof, the entire structure assembling in under a minute in experienced hands and weighing less than nine pounds.

"Timer on!" Darkwood shouted.

"Shelters up!" Paul ordered.

John Rourke and Paul Rubenstein raised the shelter above them, Michael, Darkwood, Aldridge, and all the rest of the team moving under it and the second, identical shelter brought by the second team. Rourke's eyes followed the injured German commando as he was carried in. The man's color looked better and he was visibly respirating.

"Shelters down!"

John Rourke and Paul Rubenstein turned, stepped under the shelter, and dropped to their knees, lowering the shelter over them and the others.

"Brace!" Paul ordered.

Rourke turned his back to the shelter wall, the heels of his palms going downward over the interior lip of the shelter, Michael beside him doing the same. Across from him, Rourke could see Paul, Darkwood, and Aldridge, could see them clearly, the shelter dome translucent.

Michael was counting off. "Five . . . four . . . three . . . two . . . one!"

The explosion came, Rourke ducking his head involuntarily as the fireball rolled over the dome, then a section of the ladder leading to the interior hatch lashed across the shelter's roof, the entire structure vibrating with it but keeping its integrity.

The noise stopped.

"Gas grenades!" Darkwood shouted, pulling his mask over his head, Rourke and the others doing the same, shouldering the shelter onto its side as Aldridge, a German officer, and Han Lu Chen raced to the opening beneath the porthole, bracing stubby-barreled launchers about the size of witness protection shotguns against their thighs, firing, each launcher sending an eight-inch-long gas grenade up through the well of the airlock and through the opening just made when the hatch was blown away.

The gas was odorless and tasteless, but possessed of a deep rose color. Its knockout agent would put anyone who breathed it to sleep for better than two hours, according to the German scientists.

As they fired the gas cartridges, Rourke stripped out of his chest pack and environment suit, buckling on his utility belt around the waist of the black surface suit he wore beneath the dry suit. He rammed one of the Scoremasters into his belt and drew the second one from the interior thigh holster.

Gas billowed downward now, purplish wisps of it in layers near the overhead.

"Stun grenades!" Rourke ordered, his son and his friend moving forward, hand-lobbing sound and light grenades upward through the hatch opening. Rourke rammed both Scoremasters into his utility belt. "Watch it!" Rourke averted his eyes, cupping both hands over his ears as the first of the grenades detonated.

There was a succession of high pitched, ear-splittingly loud whines, and even with his eyes squinted shut, Rourke could still detect a heightened light level for a split second.

And then it was over. As he turned around, Michael and Paul were moving under the hatchway, John Rourke right behind them. Michael and Paul dropped to their knees, Rourke climbing onto their backs, reaching up, grasping for a handhold, pulling himself up and through, careful about the ragged outline where the hatch had been blown from its flange.

Rourke pushed away a fallen body — dead — and rolled onto the deck. There was no resistance here. Rourke's left hand racked the slide of one of the Scoremasters. He upped the safety, put the gun into his belt, then racked the second pistol. He drew the first gun again.

Now Paul, then Michael, then Darkwood, then Aldridge rose out of the hatchway.

Purple smoke hung heavy everywhere around them, both fore and aft in the ready room.

A watertight doorway was shut just beyond.

"Demolition!" Aldridge ordered. "Fix that!"

"Bring that injured German up here and assign a man to stay with him," Darkwood ordered.

"Yes, sir!" Aldridge snapped back.

Rourke moved toward the doorway, Paul and Michael flanking him. Behind them, Darkwood was announcing, "Let's have more gas ready and more sound and light!"

Time was the commodity most precious to them now, Rourke realized. If the Soviets had the chance to electronically seal each watertight doorway, fighting to seize the Island Classer would be compartment by compartment, and still the Soviet commander would be able to continue launching the rest of his missile complement against New Germany.

"Stand back!" Aldridge shouted as the marine by the doorway gave a hand signal.

Rourke turned away, taking shelter beside an equipment rack.

There was the sound of a small explosion, the center of the watertight doorway blown outward, Aldridge and Han Lu Chen running up, firing gas grenades through the opening.

171

As Aldridge and Han stepped away, Michael and Paul lobbed sound and light grenades through the opening.

"Watch it!" Rourke ordered.

This time there was no need to close his eyes, just avert them. Still grasping his pistol, he covered his ears as best he could, but the remaining portion of the door effectively shielded him and the others from the largest part of the stun grenades' effect.

A German commando ran to the doorway as the sound died, stabbing the muzzle of his assault rifle through the opening, firing, turreting the weapon right and left and up and down.

A marine from Mid-Wake worked the lock mechanism, three men racing through the opening as soon as the door swung back.

John Rourke followed them, stepping over the flange and into the corridor beyond. "More gas! Lots of it!"

Two of the Germans now, along with Han and Aldridge, began firing gas grenades in both directions along the corridor.

Darkwood pointed forward and shouted, "Follow me!"

John Rourke sprinted after him, Paul and Michael running along on either side.

The corridor was interrupted at another watertight door, but this one was only closed, not locked. "Just routine during combat. So far so good," Darkwood announced.

Paul worked the locking wheel, John Rourke and his son giving cover as Han and the other three gas grenadiers fired their rounds through into the companionway beyond.

Aldridge started over the flange, but John Rourke and Michael beat him, taking up flanking positions on the opposite side of the doorway as Sam and a half dozen other men passed through.

No resistance here.

Darkwood, his issue Mid-Wake Lancer 9mm in hand, stepped over the flange. "The reactor room, gentlemen. Let's move!"

Darkwood started along the corridor in the wake of a wedge of marines led by Sam Aldridge, Rourke walking quietly after them, his son and his friend on either side of him. His knowledge of Island Class submarines was limited, but assuming their layout followed a pattern similar to that outlined in

Darkwood's briefing, the logical place for an ambush would be between the reactor complex and the crews' quarters. Access to the command deck could be restricted merely by closing a hatch access, and the commander of the Island Class submarine would assume — perhaps rightly — that an explosion could not be risked lest navigational and other instrumentation be damaged or destroyed. Fighting into the crews' quarters, or officers' quarters farther forward, could be sealed off or at least stalled by personnel in the crews' and officers' mess above.

The only danger would be that invaders would sabotage the reactor room, but the results of such an action could threaten every life aboard — officers, crew, and attackers.

John Rourke caught up with Darkwood, whispering to him, "Paul and Michael and I are taking a different route. That way, if you get boxed in, we may be able to attack from the rear."

Darkwood looked at Rourke for an instant, then nodded his head. "Good idea, Doctor. But be careful."

"See you." And Rourke dodged into a side companionway just ahead, Paul and Michael after him.

"What's up, John?"

Voices sounded oddly hollow filtered through a gas mask, and more unnerving still were the clouds of purple gas through which they walked, the gas here relatively diffused. "Darkwood and his people won't be getting slowed down by intruder defense systems, because they're all gas-related and we're masked and the surface suits protect us from skin absorption, but there should be armed resistance once they've passed into or through the reactor room. We can leave the machinery spaces and reach the science labs if I remember Darkwood's briefing well enough." He looked at Michael.

Michael nodded. "Yeah. There's an access tube. Then what?"

"From the science, it's an easy shot to medical," Paul said slowly, "and then just forward of that's the con."

"But from the back door," John Rourke added, breaking into a jogtrot down the companionway, his son and his friend with him.

173

Chapter Forty

Everywhere Natalia looked there was devastation, the main level of the National Defense Headquarters building all but destroyed, piles of rubble littering the marble floors, columns toppled, the ceiling above her head groaning, ready to collapse, as she picked her way among the piles of debris and the dead.

She quickened her pace, stopping only to check the occasional German defender who might possibly still live. None did.

The pattern of the devastation eluded her until she reached the main entrance, which led onto the central street of New Germany's capital. Black-clad Elite Corps shock troops controlled this segment of the city and were everywhere in considerable numbers. The main gates to the city — just barely visible to the naked eye from her vantage point — had been overrun.

About two hundred yards from the farthest of the Soviet positions, Natalia spied a row of tanks, parked side by side and blocking further access into the city.

As yet, there was no Soviet armor in sight. Buildings everywhere were in ruin, but she guessed the destruction was not so much from the bombardment as from the explosives the force she observed had utilized during their ground attack.

It was unlike Soviet strategy for armor to be so conspicuously absent.

She drew back, deeper into concealment, considering the alternatives.

Carefully evaluating them one at a time, then discarding them, she arrived at what seemed the only logical conclusion.

As if to support her reasoning, there began a shrieking sound, so piercingly loud that her ears ached from it. And then there was a roar, but it was lost in the sound of an explosion. The floor under her feet shook with it, the ceiling above her head beginning to collapse.

She looked into the street again.

The bombardment had not ended.

Instead, John and Darkwood's plan of assault on the Soviet Fleet had only brought about a temporary cessation. But when the missiles stopped raining down, some overzealous Elite Corps commander had ordered in his troops, thinking to beat the armor by only a few moments perhaps, to have the main gate taken and, with it, honors for his leadership.

She would have laughed if the results were not so deadly.

And now the Elite Corps unit was stranded, unable to push ahead, under the same bombardment leveled against the German defenders and unwilling to withdraw.

But, if John and Darkwood's plan was working, why had the bombardment begun again?

No answer presented itself, and the ceiling—the entire National Defense Headquarters—was about to come falling down on her. She harbored no fear for Sarah and Annie and Maria and the other women in the Leader Bunker. There was no means by which she could contact them, and she knew that there were several alternative methods for evacuating the bunker rather than coming straight up through National Defense Headquarters. And if the Leader Bunker had withstood the previous bombardment, it would withstand the collapse of the building above it.

About the bombardment's resumption, Natalia could do nothing.

But about the Elite Corps, there were always possibilities.

She edged along the partially demolished wall. The ceiling and the very walls of the National Defense Headquarters groaned, creaking around her. There was a knot of three Elite Corpsmen about thirty yards from her.

If she could kill them all before they realized the building was collapsing and ran for their lives, she had a chance—if the building's collapse didn't get her as well.

She safed the German battle weapon, pushing it behind her back on its sling. Instead, she drew the suppressor-fitted Walther PPK/S .380 from its inverted shoulder holster. The Walther clutched tight in her gloved right fist, Natalia Anastasia Tiemerovna began creeping forward to attack the Elite Corps, a unit begun five centuries ago by the husband who had tried to kill her, who had become the symbol to her of everything that was evil and vile, equally a traitor to Communism and to humanity in every form.

There was an open space of about ten feet to cross until she reached an overturned public shuttle behind which she could take cover and concealment. She ran now, keeping her body low, the Walther out ahead of her like a talisman against death.

And she started to murmur under her breath, "Fuck you, Vladmir," but the mere thought of the meaning behind the common vulgarism made Natalia shiver.

Chapter Forty-one

There was gunfire amidships now as John Rourke, Michael Rourke, and Paul Rubenstein climbed through the access tube toward the Island Classer's science bay.

The walls of the tube gleamed bright like burnished gold but were merely stainless steel or some modern equivalent, reflecting the beam of John Rourke's flashlight.

As he spotted a small hatchway ahead, Rourke hissed to Michael and Paul below him, "I think we're there." But what they would find "there" was uncertain. Had he commanded the Island Classer, John Rourke knew, he would have stationed one armed crewman at each access tube hatch throughout the aft portion of the submarine, to guard against just such a tactic.

He hoped now, as he approached the hatch, touching a gloved hand to the locking wheel, that the Soviet commander did not have such foresight.

One man with a little skill and imagination and the proper weapon could hold off twenty or more men trying to squeeze through the smallish access hatchways, merely picking them off one at a time.

Rourke secured the flashlight, one of the Detonics Scoremasters in his right fist, his left hand on the wheel. "Be ready," he rasped to his son and his friend.

John Rourke's left hand began to move the wheel, which squeaked in response. "Damn," he hissed. But John Rourke had planned ahead. From one of the pouches on his belt, he took a tube of lubricant. Belting his pistol for a moment, he notched the end of the tube with his knife. Resheathing the knife, he applied the lubricant liberally to the hub of the wheel.

Rourke waited, the distant sound of gunfire unabated.

It was hot inside the gas mask, but he could take no chances with the Island Classer's intruder defense system, gas weapons at the very minimum.

Rourke convinced himself that sufficient time had elapsed for the synth lube to penetrate. He drew one of the Scoremasters and again tried the wheel.

No squeak.

The wheel turned quickly, and as it neared the end of its rotation, Rourke gave it a hard twist, released it, then drew his second Scoremaster. The wheel stopped.

The door opened slowly under Rourke's hand pressure, the second Scoremaster held loosely in his fingers.

John Rourke peered out into the science labs. There was no one immediately in evidence and he swung his body around, getting his feet through, then jumped, coming down in a crouch, the hammers of both Scoremasters rolling back under his thumbs.

Behind him, he heard the sounds of Michael and Paul exiting the access tube, the scuffing of feet, the creaking of equipment, the cocking of the hammer on Paul's battered Browning High Power.

The compartment into which they'd entered was long and narrow, on second glance quite clearly an interior corridor connecting sections of the science labs to each other, watertight doors on either side. These were closed. John Rourke signaled Paul and Michael back, approaching the nearer of these two doors, the one on his right.

Rourke flattened himself against the interior bulkhead. He extended his right leg, then gently nudged his foot against the door. It held fast. Rourke signaled to Paul and Michael, but they were already coming up, taking positions on either side of him. Rourke touched at the wheel of the watertight door, the second Scoremaster safed and slipped into his belt.

The wheel spun easily. Anyone on the other side of the doorway would realize the door was being opened, so there was no need for perfect silence.

As soon as the lock cleared, Rourke redrew the .45 and kicked against the door, stepping back and right.

Through the open doorway, he could see no one. Paul and

Michael went through the doorway, Paul crossing left to right, Michael right to left. Rourke followed them, dodging right as he entered.

The laboratory was deserted. At its far end was a winding metal staircase, connecting, Rourke deduced, science to medical above.

"Let's go," Rourke almost whispered, starting for the stairs. . . .

There was another high-pitched whistling whine. Another missile would be striking the mountain at any second. The National Defense Headquarters would collapse, or at least partially so, and the three men who were her targets—she was less than fifteen feet from them—would run for their lives.

She waited, although it was hard for her to do so. But Natalia waited for the whine of the incoming missile to be at its loudest.

As it crescendoed, she rose from her position of concealment behind the overturned transport, the Walther PPK/S American in both fists. She fired once, into the axial vertebrae of the farthest of the three Elite Corpsmen, killing him instantly, his body slapping forward. She swung the suppressor-fitted muzzle of the Walther and fired again, into the left ear of the man second farthest from her. The third man was turning around, bringing his assault rifle up. Natalia shot him in the right eye. She wheeled back to the second man, putting another bullet into his head.

The missile impacted, Natalia thrown to the ground by the shock wave, huge slabs of building material crashing downward, the street in front of her buckling upward, a water main rupturing.

Natalia pushed herself to her feet and ran, jumping the widening crack in the street and coming down in a roll. She got to her feet again, running as the crack widened toward her.

She reached the smallest of the three dead men, grabbed his body by the collar of his BDUs, and dragged him after her, the crack splitting the street wide open, one of the two bodies fall-

179

ing into it, the water spray covering everything now. . . .

At the height of the stairs, the medical complex was not on alert, and there were six med-techs involved in day-to-day routines. As Rourke came out of the stairwell and trained both Scoremasters on them, he called out in Russian for them to remain just where they were and they would not be hurt.

Six sets of arms were raised at once.

The most humane thing was to use one of the gas grenades, which could either be fired from a grenade launcher as before or merely thrown. Rourke cautioned the six to lie down as comfortably as possible and breathe deeply.

Within seconds, all six were unconscious and, aside from colossal headaches, would be none the worse for wear when they awakened.

Rourke went to a supply cabinet, found a large plastic bottle of Soviet acetaminophen tablets, then set it on one of the tables near where the six lay.

Rourke looked at Paul, who was checking the German MP-40 which, after all this time, he still called a "Schmiesser." Michael was substituting twenty-round magazines in his Beretta 92Fs. John Rourke shrugged his shoulders under the weight of the double Alessi shoulder rig's harness, then checked the little Centennial .38 he'd brought along.

He picked up both Scoremasters—cocked and locked—from the table nearest him. "Gentlemen?"

"Ready," Paul nodded.

"Ready," Michael almost whispered.

"I'll get the door," Paul volunteered, then broke into a jog trot across the medical complex toward the watertight door at the far end.

Beyond it, there should be a companionway, which would likely be guarded at the other end, because it led directly to the Con at the heart of the Command Deck.

Rourke started across the medical section, his son falling in beside him. . . .

* * *

The man's clothes fit Natalia well enough but, like many Russians of her own day, he had not bathed frequently enough and had covered his body odor with cologne, from which the clothes now positively reeked. What blood had begun coagulating on the collar of the BDU blouse she was able to rub off easily because the dead Elite Corpsman's clothing, like her own, was soaked in the spray from the ruptured, still-spouting water main.

Her wet hair at last satisfactorily stuffed under the Elite Corpsman's BDU cap — she'd checked for head lice and found none — Natalia crawled out of the shadow of the pile of building rubble, the Soviet assault rifle in her hands.

Fires burned around the city, she guessed as the result of electrical disruption. Grey-blue trailers of synth fuel hung heavy on the air.

The Elite Corps front line was now a ragged crescent, and after the last missile strike, small arms fire had erupted between the Soviet and German units closest to each other. The German tanks held their line, and as yet there was no Soviet armor rolling through the Soviet-held main entrance to the German capital.

Of machine gun emplacements on the Soviet side, she saw only five, this reinforcing her opinion that the Elite Corps unit's commander had decided to hit fast, traveling light. Glancing toward the main entrance again, she could almost visualize their strike. Evidently, one or more of the missiles had wiped out much of the German defense immediately outside the main entrance. While that was being reorganized and with the missile attack temporarily ceased, this unit — only a few hundred men at most — had been sent in.

"Idiot," Natalia murmured in English, shaking her head. The sort of field commander who would send in that many men with so few heavier weapons to back them up against a fortified position such as this displayed total lack of concern for the lives of those men.

What she needed to do was reach one of the machine guns, preferably the most rearward of them, and hope that once she started using it the Germans would counterattack. If she could hold out long enough . . . Natalia licked her lips, wishing for a cigarette.

She pulled the visor of her cap lower over her eyes. She looked down her front, making certain the purse she had stuffed in over her chest to disguise her figure was where it should be. That the material from which the black bag was made was also bullet resistant was at least a little comforting.

Holding the rifle in both hands, she started running forward in a low crouch, to join the comrades attacking New Germany. . . .

The watertight door opening onto the main upper deck companionway was along the leg of the companionway, an L-shape, not directly opposite the watertight door leading to the Island Classer's Con.

John Rourke, with Paul and Michael just behind him, edged along the interior bulkhead, past more medical facilities, no time to worry about who might or might not be working inside.

At the terminus of the L's leg to the main section of the companionway, John Rourke stopped.

Among Paul, Michael, and himself, there were eight gas grenades remaining. Rourke popped one grenade free from his equipment belt, Michael doing the same. He signaled Paul to save his remaining two.

John Rourke edged closer to the corner where the two segments of companionway met and drew the small mirror from the breast pocket of his surface suit. Angling it, he could see along the companionway toward the watertight door. As he'd suspected, the door was guarded, four men with assault rifles and a two-man machine gun team.

All six men wore gas masks.

Sporadic gunfire could be heard coming from at least one deck below.

Rourke replaced his gas grenades, useless now. "Hold off on the gas," he hissed through his mask. "Sound and light first, then guns. They're wearing masks. Paul, lob two sound and lights. That'll leave you one. I've got one and so does Michael." Paul nodded, snapping two sound and light grenades from his

182

equipment, pulling the pin on first one, then the other. Michael positioned himself with both Berettas to cover Paul.

John Rourke checked the mirror one last time. "Now," he whispered.

Paul Rubenstein snapped both sound and light grenades down the companionway, pulling back, Rourke bringing both hands up to his ears as the machine gun opened up, Michael drawing back as his father closed his eyes against the flash.

As the whine of the grenades died, Rourke stabbed both Scoremasters around the corner, firing three shots from each, up and down and side to side, Michael firing both Berettas from shoulder level as he dodged into the companionway, then back.

Paul Rubenstein had the submachine gun up, hosing it empty down the companionway, making a fast tactical change with the magazines, the second one already ready. He nodded.

John Rourke stepped into the companionway, both pistols ahead of him, firing at everything that moved. Crouched beside him, Paul fired the submachine gun from the shoulder, the stock extended. Michael moved slowly forward along the companionway, both Berettas firing.

One of the machine gun team was still moving. John Rourke fired the last round from the Scoremaster in his right hand, putting the man down.

At point-blank range, Michael killed the last of the six men, then framed himself against the bulkhead to the right of the watertight door.

Rourke, his friend beside him, ran the length of the companionway, changing magazines in the Scoremasters, Paul changing magazines in the German MP-40.

The watertight door would be locked and it made no sense to even try it.

While Paul and Michael scrounged weapons from the dead, John Rourke took the magnetic mine from the pack on his son's back and clamped it near the locking mechanism.

Paul, the Soviet light machine gun leaned against the bulkhead near him, started the rope of plastique-like explosive, feeding it out of its protective tube as Michael molded the

183

substance into the juncture of watertight door and flange.

John Rourke had two of the Soviet assault rifles now, fresh forty-round magazines loaded. He moved back along the companionway, gas spraying from small jets where the bulkheads on either side of the companionway met the overhead.

The gas was grey as fog and billowed downward in thick clouds.

Michael shouted, "Ready!"

"Now!" John Rourke called back.

Michael and Paul raced back along the companionway, drawing into shelter in the leg of the "L" beside Rourke as the first explosion came, the second one—louder—just after it.

The manner in which the explosives were set would result in a Misme-Chardin effect with the watertight door, propelling it inward and across the Con. But John Rourke had planned ahead. The same explosion from beneath the Con level or from forward would have destroyed most of the submarine's instrumentation, but from aft it would knock out the actual Con itself, along with the periscope array—he hoped.

Otherwise, he had just made a derelict of the Island Classer, one they might not even be able to surface.

John Rourke stepped into the companionway, breaking into a run for the doorway opening, a jagged maw now, smoke rising around it still. And Paul was beside him, firing the Soviet LMG in controlled bursts, high through the doorway opening.

Paul neared the doorway, firing the LMG up and down, right and left. Michael fired a burst from each assault rifle he held.

Rourke reached the twisted flange and jumped it, one of the Soviet rifles in each fist. Crew personnel lay everywhere, bodies twisted and torn. Small arms fire emanated now from the height of a circular stairwell just beyond the command chair, the Soviet commander lying dead in his seat.

Marine Spetznas holding off Darkwood's people below, John Rourke returned fire, Paul edging right to maximize on the LMG's effect and minimize equipment damage, Michael moving forward beside his father, their assault rifles spraying controlled bursts into the stairwell. Gunfire from below the level of the command deck increased. There was the sound of a gas grenade exploding, purple translucent fingers of gas extending upward within the stairwell.

John Rourke let one of the assault rifles fall to his side on its sling, tearing one of the sound and light grenades from his gear, shouting through the mask he wore, "Egg!" He pitched the grenade down the stairwell, averting his eyes, doing the best he could to protect his ears from the sound, the whine painfully loud. As it began to subside, his ears still ringing from it, Rourke moved ahead.

A Marine Spetznas, obviously temporarily blinded, ran out of the stairwell, firing an assault rifle, spraying bullets everywhere. Rourke got him with two short bursts from one of the Soviet rifles, putting him down dead.

Shoulder to shoulder now, John Rourke, flanked by his son and his friend, advanced across the Con. From below, he could faintly hear Jason Darkwood ordering, "Follow me!"

Chapter Forty-two

Natalia huddled from German small arms fire in the midst of a dozen Elite Corpsmen. Fewer than ten yards separated her from the nearest of the five Soviet machine guns. From the gear of the three dead men, one of whose uniforms she wore, she had three grenades.

The dozen men surrounding her were the problem now — the men and the time. The missile bombardment had apparently ceased, and if this were indeed a signal for the full-scale Soviet ground attack, in a few more minutes all would be lost unless the main entrance could be retaken. She pushed away thoughts of what had happened to Sarah and Annie and Maria and the other women in the aftermath of the collapse of the National Defense Headquarters, and what fate might have befallen John and Paul and Michael and the others who had gone to assault the Soviet submarines laying the bombardment.

She focused her thoughts now on killing the twelve men surrounding her and reaching the machine gun emplacement. She had one assault rifle only, and even had she two of the weapons, she could not hope to take out all twelve men before at least one of them opened fire and killed her.

And then a smile crossed her lips.

Crouching lower as the German small arms fire conveniently increased in volume, Natalia took one of the Soviet grenades from her equipment harness. It was similar in outward design to the American baseball grenades of five centuries ago. A cotter pin of some plastic material kept the spoon attached to the body. She glanced over her shoulders on either side, her "comrades" clustered in small groups, some returning fire, most hiding behind cover.

The Bali-Song.

She opened it slowly so there wouldn't be any noise. Inverting the grenade, propping it over a fragment of paving from the street, she levered downward with the Bali-Song's primary edge, cutting through the plastic cotter pin, leaving its end flush against the juncture with the spoon so no pin showed.

She closed the Bali-Song now and pocketed it, drew the issue bayonet from her gear, then wedged it beneath the handle of the spoon, between the handle and the grenade's body. She pried upward, her right hand squeezed hard around the bayonet's hilt. "Let it be pot metal," she almost prayed.

The bayonet was starting to bend, but the spoon handle snapped, flicking away.

Without hesitating, Natalia rolled the harmless grenade into the midst of the men around her, making her voice as deep as she could when she shouted, "Grenade! Run, comrades!"

She started to run, glancing back, the men who'd been around her dispersing in all directions.

Two men ran in the direction of the machine gun emplacement.

Natalia fired her assault rifle in two short bursts, killing them, German small arms fire rippling across the pavement near her feet. One of the men behind the machine gun raised up, stabbing a pistol toward her. She fired, stitching him from abdomen to throat.

The second man in the machine gun team swung the weapon toward her.

Natalia fired again, a long burst into his neck and face, knocking his body back. She threw herself toward the machine gun.

Two Elite Corps men charged toward her.

She pulled one of the Smith & Wesson L-Frames from beneath her BDU blouse and shot one man in the chest, the second in the neck, stabbing the revolver into her waistband as she swung the machine gun on line with the nearest knot of Elite Corpsmen and opened fire, spraying the machine gun across their position, killing or wounding nine of them. She swung the muzzle of the machine gun, firing long bursts at every Elite Corps position within reach, firing, firing.

And she screamed in German, "Attack! Attack!"

Natalia swept the hat back from her head, her hair cascading down, her right finger pressed against the machine gun's trigger. . . .

Jason Darkwood said, "Well, not in perfect condition, granted, but I think we can establish contact with the other two Island Classers. Michael, why don't you?"

"Right," Michael Rourke nodded.

Jason Darkwood added, "Make sure to find out, Michael, which submarine may have our people in control and which may have a Soviet commander still at the helm."

"Okay, Jason."

Darkwood merely shook his head, John Rourke watching him. Darkwood's face would have been amusing—just seeing how the man was trying to cope with a bridge crew of largely inept amateurs—except that the survival of New Germany and the Allied cause depended on whether or not he could get the Island Classer's missiles turned against the Soviet land forces while at the same time avoiding a battle with one or both Island Classers near them.

Darkwood turned to Sam Aldridge. "How are we on weapon's systems, Sam?"

"We've got a full complement of cluster charges to port and starbord, and a full complement of torpedoes fore and aft, and nineteen missiles remaining. None of the warheads nuclear, as far as I can tell, Jase."

Darkwood said. "Very well. Adjust targeting to the last available coordinates for the Soviet land force. All of the missiles."

"Yes, sir!"

Han Lu Chen, at the sonar console, volunteered, "As far as I could tell, Captain Darkwood, one of the Soviet undersea boats has turned around."

" 'Coming about' is the proper terminology, Mr. Han."

Michael Rourke sang out, "Jason, I've got confirmation that the Island Classer nearest to us is in Allied hands. Evidently, the third team got stopped."

Jason Darkwood looked down at his hands, and whispered, "There were a lot of good men in that third team. Shit. Mr. Rourke, if your Russian can manage it, signal the third Island Classer to surrender now. No terms except that their lives will be spared. Period. Don't wait for a response. On the same frequency, signal Island Classer number two to prepare to fire starboard side cluster charges on my command. The full complement, and prepare for firing torpedoes fore and aft at their discretion."

"But will they know how?"

"Of course not," Darkwood told Michael Rourke, "but the Russians won't know that."

"I'm on it," Michael shouted back.

Darkwood turned to Paul Rubenstein, at the engineering console. "Mr. Rubenstein, how's it coming getting some control over this little submarine we've inherited?"

Paul, crouched beneath the console, called back, "I think I've got enough things wired together that we have a full range of motion, Jason."

Darkwood nodded, saying, "Very good, Mr. Rubenstein. Be ready to push the right buttons and pull the right switches when I indicate." Darkwood turned to Michael Rourke again, saying, "Repeat the command again for surrender; don't wait for response; make a big show of talking to Island Classer number two about releasing that full complement of starboard side cluster charges in the next twenty seconds. Then listen for Island Classer number three to surrender — I hope." He looked at Sam Aldridge. "Sam, you ready to fire some of those missiles at the Soviet ground force position?"

"Whenever you're ready."

Darkwood looked at John Rourke, asking, "Doctor, do you have indicator lights showing that we're basically in one piece enough to fire a missile without ripping ourselves apart?"

John Rourke smiled, saying, "I have green lights on all watertight doors linking major compartments" — he glanced at the weapons station, then looked back at Darkwood — "and fore and aft torpedo tubes all show to be sealed."

Darkwood looked at the watch on his left wrist, asking, "Michael, any word from our Soviet neighbors?"

Michael answered, "Nothing yet . . . hey! Wait a minute! Yeah, I'm getting a message now from Island Classer three that they are standing down."

Darkwood called back, "Order Island Classer number three to cease all navigation at once and order Islander Classer number two to keep those cluster charges ready to fire. Also, they should be prepared to fire torpedoes as necessary should the Island Classer recommence navigation." He looked at Sam Aldridge, saying, "Sam, let's pound hell out of that Soviet land force. Fire those missiles one every sixty seconds until I say otherwise."

There was dead silence on the bridge and then the Island Classer seemed to vibrate as the first missile fired.

John Rourke watched the engineering station. The submarine was holding together if the readouts were correct. . . .

As Germans swarmed toward her position, Natalia stood up, throwing both hands in the air, shouting in German to them, "I am Major Tiemerovna! I am Major Tiemerovna! Do not shoot!"

German Long Range Mountain Patrol personnel formed a ring around her, faces startled, guns lowering, a man pushing through, calling to her, "Fräulein Major! I salute you!" It was Colonel Mann, his usually impeccable uniform smoke-smudged, his hat gone, an assault rifle in his hands. "Missiles are striking Soviet positions where troops were massed for assault on the city. Three of my armored units are blocking entry to the city. The Soviet commanders can only withdraw toward the sea!"

"John," Natalia whispered.

And she sank to her knees and started to laugh, tears rimming her eyes. . . .

John Rourke stood on the deck of the Island Classer, sea spray washing over her bow as he focused his binoculars toward shore.

J7-Vs crisscrossed the beach and German helicopters

190

swarmed out of the setting sun.

All three Island Class submarines were now in Allied hands, Jason Darkwood commanding and essentially navigating all three from the Con of this one on which John Rourke stood, renamed *The Freedom* and, unofficially, the first vessel in an Allied Navy.

Soviet land force units not already destroyed by conventionally armed missiles fired from the Island Class submarine *Freedom* were withdrawing under the pressure of German armor and air power, withdrawing toward the sea.

They would have no choice but to surrender or die.

Rourke turned up the collar of his borrowed coat, inhaling smoke from the thin, dark tobacco cigar clamped in the left corner of his mouth, the binoculars hanging now from his neck.

Radio transmissions from the mountain city indicated that Sarah, Annie, and Maria, as well as the other women who had been in the Leader Bunker, were alive and well, despite the destruction of National Defense Headquarters above the bunker. Evacuation was even now underway.

And Natalia rode with Colonel Mann, Wolfgang Mann personally commanding his forces as they pressed the Germans toward the sea. Soon all three Island Class submarines would depart for the Soviet Underwater City, to aid in interdicting — God willing — Soviet nuclear retaliation. Already, Mid-Wake vessels — the *Reagan*, the *Wayne*, the captured Island Classer *Roy Rogers*, and others — were ringing the Soviets, containing only — or hoping to — until the full strike would be launched.

That would be within days, a two-pronged strike against both the underwater Soviet complex and the heart of Soviet power in the Urals. And that would end it, one way or the other, Rourke realized.

But, for another hour or so, John Thomas Rourke had nothing to do but watch the sunset and the preparations for terminating this skirmish in what might still become Armageddon.

Chapter Forty-three

There had been a few skirmishes but nothing more, the majority of the Soviet land force surrendering without significant resistance when faced with German air power above, German troops on the ground behind them, and the captured Soviet Island Classers along the shore.

The problem of what to do with prisoners was a significant one. After seizing the Cons of two of the Soviet Island Class submarines, then flooding all compartments with the very gas the Soviets utilized as an intruder defense system — a knock-out gas, nonlethal — the question of handling significant numbers of prisoners had first reared its head. After the surrender of a major Soviet land force, the situation became critical.

Camps were being set up, the problems of sanitation and medical care wrestled with, security for the camps surprisingly the easiest of the complexly interlocking issues with which to deal. There was a valley some thirty miles inland from the coast, the climate benign enough because of low elevation, the surrounding ground high with clear fields of view. Minimal numbers of troops would be required to contain vast numbers of prisoners.

John Rourke, with Paul Rubenstein beside him, stood on a grassy slope overlooking a level area about the size of ten football fields, the valley where hourly more and more of the captured Soviet combatants were arriving only a few miles farther inland.

Twelve devices, each about the size and shape of a U.S. M-60 machine gun from the days Before the Night of The War, were being taken up into the hands of twelve persons, two among these Michael and Natalia.

All of the objects were hand-fabricated. Cost, Rourke mused, had to have been enormous, but under the circumstances was wholly academic.

In all, there were twenty-four of the rather unwieldy shoulder-fired energy weapons, each powered by a back pack unit which, with John Rourke's limited knowledge of physics, seemed to closely approach the idea of harnessing naturally occurring plasma energy, as seen in ordinary lightning and ball lightning. And, there was a certain irony to this that escaped neither Rourke nor, he felt, his friend Paul Rubenstein, as they watched this second round of field testing.

"It's interesting to see Michael firing that weapon, isn't it, John? Lightning harnessed in his hands, yet it was lightninglike energy as the result of the ionization effect which nearly destroyed his world five centuries ago."

"By plasma energy, mankind was nearly undone. Now, by plasma energy, mankind may yet be saved." John Rourke nodded. He lit a cigar, watching the simple synth-fuel-powered flame of his battered Zippo. And synth fuel, after all, was nothing more than a synthetic copy of naturally occurring fossil fuel, a wheel striking a natural piece of flint, making a spark, igniting that fuel, and fire being tamed, at man's command for his every whim.

No less amazing and nearly as basic in their obedience to the laws of nature, really, were these energy weapons. And, aside from the triggering device, they were no more mechanical than his Zippo.

Only the triggering mechanism was mechanical.

Based on the original Soviet Particle Beam technology developed in the years before The Night of The War, which was never fully implemented, the plasma energy had initially been used to accelerate particles. But with this current technology, the plasma energy itself became the weapon.

It was based on the theory of the glow discharge . . . the inverse of the principle utilized in magnetohydrodynamic power generation. By pulsing magnetic fields in the plasma, beams of energy in relation to the square of the magnetic field were achieved. The glow discharge occurred between two electrodes. Whereas during The Great Conflagration, high amounts of plasma energy from enormously powerful currents in the ionized atmosphere all but destroyed the planet, the glow discharge based on a comparatively minimal current produced a degree of ionization that was controllable, and in conjunction with a rather imaginative application of Landau Damping to control wave amplitude, the result was a gun that discharged lightning bolts, rather like the shepherds of ancient Greece had imagined were hurled by an angry Zeus.

Ionizing the electrons near the cathode within the system activated plasma near the anode. What originally had charged ions for partical beam weaponry and was still being used by the Russians to generate laser beams now was able to combine the more conventional glow discharge into the more spectacular electric discharge arc. In chemistry or physics, the implications of such practical technology were nearly beyond Rourke's imagining — everything from drive systems for spacecraft to an infinite power supply bypassing the traditional steam/mechanical engine. But the potential of this energy as a weapon was crystal clear.

Within months, at an accelerated rate of development, the power supply pack would be miniaturized, and rather than the ungainly shoulder-fired weapons being tested in this deserted field outside the German mountain city, there would be hand and shoulder weapons as convenient as cartridges in the high-capacity 9mm pistols and 5.56mm assault rifles in use five centuries ago.

The age of the "ray gun" had arrived.

John Rourke watched his son as the range was called safe for firing and Michael raised his weapon, took aim, and fired on a man-sized silhouette some two hundred meters distant. There was a laser sighting device mounted to the energy weapon, and if the laser beam could be settled on the target clearly enough to be seen, the target could be hit. In bright light, as was the case now, an optical sight built into the carrying handle was utilized. Michael leaned into the weapon and fired. A lightning bolt — pale blue in color and almost blindingly bright — discharged from the weapon's muzzle, striking the target.

"Welcome to the future," Paul observed.

"Yes, but ours or theirs?" And John Rourke nodded his head inland, toward the valley in which the Soviet prisoners were to be held until this war reached its inevitable conclusion. Just what that conclusion might be, who would win, was subject of so many variables that a scenario for its outcome was not readily apparent.

And if the Soviets launched nuclear weapons from their enclave beneath the Pacific, there would be no world remaining at all.

John Rourke examined the glowing tip of his cigar.

Chapter Forty-four

John Rourke stared down into the water thousands of feet below the J7-V in which he rode. It was the wrong ocean, of course, the Atlantic rather than the Pacific, but he could imagine Jason Darkwood piloting the new Allied Fleet of commandeered Soviet Island Class submarines toward a rendezvous in the Pacific with the men of Mid-Wake.

But John Rourke's affairs took him elsewhere. Jason Darkwood and the United States Marines of Mid-Wake, plus a core group of Allied Commandos, would assault the Soviet underwater facility in the Pacific, to interdict Soviet nuclear strike capability in support of Soviet land forces headquartered out of the Underground City in the Urals. And the Ural Mountains of Soviet Europe were John Rourke's ultimate destination.

First, a strike at Antonovitch's field HQ near where, five centuries ago, the Volga River had met the Caspian Sea. But the bombings had altered the course of the Volga, and the entire area from what had been the bed of the Volga to the still-flowing Ural River was now icy desert.

The Soviet Union's greatest airfield was there, as well as the greatest concentration of personnel and equipment outside of the Underground City itself. At Gur'yev were assembled the armies once commanded by Natalia's now-dead husband, Vladmir Karamatsov. At Gur'yev was the headquarters for the KGB Elite Corps. At Gur'yev were five armored battalions and two armored missile battalions.

With Gur'yev, there was no hope to counter the Soviet war machine.

Without Gur'yev, there was a chance.

Twenty-four operational plasma energy weapons against how many dozens or hundreds, perhaps . . . John Rourke looked away from the water, studying the charts on the screen of the German lap-top computer.

There was no other way than the way he had decided upon when first presented with the tactical difficulties involved.

John Rourke closed his eyes.

Chapter Forty-five

They sat around a rectangular folding table of considerable length. Natalia Tiemerovna studied the faces there. Wolfgang Mann looked exceedingly tired, spread too thin, much like the nation of New Germany he served. Paul looked almost anxious to be under way. Like her, with five centuries of warfare coming to a close, the prospect of peace — regardless of the dangers inherent in securing it — was so tantalizing that . . . She averted her gaze from Paul as he looked up. They exchanged the briefest of smiles.

Michael. How like his father he seemed, growing more like John every day. And not just in looks — Michael Rourke had his father's eyes, the high forehead and healthy shock of brown hair, the lined, lean face — but in his manner and his growing maturity.

John. John smoked a cigar, after first ascertaining that his smoking would not offend. He seemed unchanged — except for a little grey — from the way he had looked when she'd first opened her eyes and seen him staring down at her in the Texas desert five centuries ago, unchanged from when she'd seen him that very first time in Latin America when he was still active CIA.

That very first time, he'd worn a white dinner jacket, looking ridiculously handsome. In the West Texas desert, he'd worn a light blue chambray shirt and faded jeans. This time, he was dressed in black — black knit shirt, black BDU pants, black lace-up-the-front boots.

And now John spoke, and the eyes of every man in the room — she was the only woman — settled upon him. These were tough men, hardened fighters, German Long Range Mountain Patrol commanders, German Commandos like Otto Hammerschmidt, men like First Chinese City Intelligence Commando Han Lu Chen and Icelandic policeman Bjorn Rolvaag.

"A portion of our force under the command of United States Marine Captain Sam Aldridge will attack Gur'yev from the northern shore of the Caspian as a separate element, but that attack will not commence until our job at the base has been taken care of. When Aldridge and his force — they're all Mid-Wake Marines and skilled at diving procedures and have trained as much as time has allowed in lightning-fast penetrations against shore-based targets — but when they hit, they'll knock out the anti-aircraft emplacements along the shore itself. Our task is two-fold.

"Major Tiemerovna, Paul Rubenstein, my son Michael, and I will penetrate within the base itself. Meanwhile, Captain Otto Hammerschmidt — ohh, I'm sorry, Major Hammerschmidt of late," and John nodded deferentially toward Otto Hammerschmidt, recently promoted. "Major Hammerschmidt and Mr. Han, meanwhile, with the assistance of Officer Rolvaag, will lead an attack against the second of the two primary anti-aircraft facilities, this to the north of the Gur'yev base. Their task will be relatively similar to that of Captain Aldridge — to knock out the anti-aircraft defenses so that after Natalia, Paul, Michael, and I have done our work, German paratroops can hit the main portion of the base itself, under the command of Major Hartmann, also recently promoted." And again John nodded, this time at Hartmann, de facto field commander for the German forces in Europe. "As Major Hartmann's personnel strike, Colonel Mann will personally lead a force of J7-Vs and helicopters against the base.

"Just as important as knocking out the anti-aircraft facilities is preventing as many Soviet aircraft as possible from scrambling, getting airborne. That is the task Natalia, Michael, Paul, and I will undertake. From the Soviet prisoners taken during the fighting in New Germany, we've been able to assemble uniforms. From Soviet ID and orders, technicians at New Germany have been able to produce identical duplicate identification and cut new orders that will cover the four of us getting into the base. We hope."

There was a hint of subdued, very forced laughter.

John went on. "Natalia's Russian is perfect and mine is good. If we were going against the Soviet underwater complex, we'd have greater problems because the progress of the Russian language there over the centuries since The Night of the War has been considerably different and the Russian spoken there is a distinctly different-sounding dialect. Both Paul and Michael have acquired a sufficient amount of Russian to carry on basic conversations, and both of them understand more than they command as a spoken vocabulary. So we should be all right in that department as well. With uniforms, ID papers, orders, and the language, unless we are recognized by some other means, we'll make it onto the base.

"Once into the base, we'll proceed to the airfield." John reached into a musette bag on the table in front of him, opening a jewelrylike box and taking from it what appeared to be an ordinary issue Soviet military wristwatch. "Each of the four of us will have one of these, in the event we are separated or something else unforeseen arises to keep us from functioning together as a unit. Once again"—and John nodded toward Colonel Mann—"we can thank German technological ingenuity. These are Soviet wristwatches on the outside, and like their more normal counterparts they tell time—not too well." There was laughter, John smiling. "They indicate temperature, barometric pressure, and background radiation readings. Unlike the actual issue watches, however, each of these is equipped with a one-time-only use radio transmitting device."

John demonstrated, removing his Rolex Submariner, then placing the Soviet watch on his wrist in its stead. As he took the watch away from his wrist, he turned it so the segment of the band with the locking clasp was upward. "The band itself looks synthetic, like those used on the Soviet issue watch, but is, rather, a metal alloy. It will serve as a projection antenna for the radio signaling device which is actuated by pulling the stem outward past the set position and then winding it."

There were blank looks on the faces of everyone in the room except for Paul and Michael. "In the days prior to battery-operated watches," John explained, "watches were mechanical. My watch, for example, is what was called 'self-winding.' Merely picking up a Rolex once a day will keep it running. But

200

more basic watches required that at least once in every twenty-four-hour period the stem of the watch — as the Soviets use here merely for setting — had to be rotated back and forth until spring tension was such that the stem could be rotated, or wound, no further without forcing it. 'Winding.' We will wind the watch until it achieves maximum tension, and when that tension releases, the radio signal will have fired. That signal, from Natalia's or Michael's or Paul's or my Soviet watch, will be received — we hope, again — by Colonel Mann's forces. At that time, a drone J7-V will overfly Gur'yev field and bomb it. The drone will be shot down, most likely, but whether it is or isn't, the resultant dislocation should provide cover for us to reach our primary objective with the explosives we'll be carrying. Then we have to blow up a bunch of aircraft."

"How will you escape the base, Doctor?" Han Lu Chen asked.

"We will take up the best defensive position available and wait it out until Major Hartmann's paratroopers reach the field. We will then don armbands — blaze orange ones — by which means we will hopefully be distinguishable from enemy personnel. And, if all goes even moderately well, we neutralize Gur'yev base and move on to the Underground City for a coordinated strike timed to coincide with Mid-Wake's submarine and commando attack on the Soviet underwater complex in the Pacific."

Natalia lit a cigarette, not bothering to ask if her smoking would bother anyone. If John's cigar hadn't produced that result, her cigarette was certainly safe.

The moment she'd been waiting for for so long was nearly at hand.

This sole obstacle — Gur'yev — was all that remained before a final confrontation that would end it, one way or the other.

She exhaled, watching the smoke from her cigarette drift upward toward the ceiling of the environmentally controlled tent.

And she was suddenly very lonely, because however this turned out — whether she lay dead in some anonymous mass grave or survived to be free — to be alone was her destiny forever.

Chapter Forty-six

He was a major of the KGB Elite Corps, according to his borrowed black uniform, the bullet hole that had been in the chest of the last man who'd worn it rewoven in New Germany by removing a patch of material from the crotch of the uniform trousers and replacing it with a similar, but not identical piece of fabric.

If one of the guards at Gur'yev got close enough to check for the patch in the crotch, its discovery would be the least of John Rourke's worries.

To disguise his appearance, he'd shaved away most of his sideburns. Anticipating such a penetration into the Soviet sphere of influence, he had not shaved his upper lip for the last two weeks, the resultant mustache — a little grey — serving to draw his features downward, making his already naturally long face seem that much longer.

Beside John Rourke, the only one of the four of them wearing appropriate rank, sat Natalia. She was uniformed as a female major of the KGB Elite Corps, which she had been — KGB, at least.

Despite the severity of the uniform — knee-length black A-line skirt, heavy stockings, and sensible shoes under an open ankle-length greatcoat — she looked exquisite, as was normal for her in any event. Her almost-black hair was covered with a blond wig, considerably shorter than her own hair beneath it, so short it was almost the length of a man's hair.

In the front seat of the Soviet ATV staff car, on the driver's side, Paul was uniformed as a senior sergeant. Beside him, hair dyed blond and fake mustache added to divert the casual observer from the obvious physical similarities between son and father, Michael was uniformed as a lieutenant.

As Paul slowed the staff ATV to take the deliberate right

angle onto the roadway leading toward the main gate, John Rourke checked under his uniform blouse. With some skillful tailoring by quartermaster personnel at New Germany, he was able to conceal his twin stainless Detonics CombatMasters in the double Alessi shoulder rig, a supressor-fitted 6906 in a specially designed inner pocket of his greatcoat and the two Scoremasters in his belt.

The little Centennial was in the outside pocket of his great-coat, ideal for that application because the hammer was completely enclosed and there was absolutely nothing to foul in the pocket lining if the gun were to be discharged.

And he smiled now as he remembered the words of his old friend, master gunsmith and consummate martial artist Ron Mahovsky, concerning his lifelong addiction to the revolver. "Six for sure." The Centennial was only "five for sure," but the principle was the same.

"We're going to be stopping in a minute or so for the first gate check," Paul advised.

"Remember the Soviet Communist weltanschauung," Natalia said, lighting a cigarette and exhaling a thin stream of smoke through her lips. "There is a terrifying, often paralyzing fear of authority. Constituted authority is the father figure, and in conflict with such a father figure there is always the risk of being disciplined. If we establish ourselves instantly as authority figures with which to be dealt and of which to be afraid, we can ride in easily using our cover identities and altered appearances."

"Once we're inside," John Rourke cautioned, "no matter what happens, one of us has to get to the airfield. If all hope of sabotaging a sufficient number of the aircraft themselves is lost, then we blow the synth-fuel dump. At least that will keep them from making too many sorties and tie up a lot of their ground personnel."

"If we can make it through the gates, we can make it to the airfield," Michael concluded soberly.

Rourke caught his son's eyes in the rearview mirror, their color having been altered with contact lenses and nearly the color of Sarah's eyes now. "I'm glad you're so confident. Often confidence — not overconfidence, which can net just the opposite—is the key to success."

The staff ATV began slowing.

There were heavily armed sentries on either side of the roadway, deflection barriers behind them. Sandbagged machine gun nests flanked the road on the outer side of the first segment of the security gauntlet and beyond the deflection barriers, between the outer and inner guard stations.

The gates themselves were made of solid metal, titanium Rourke guessed, twelve feet high, topped for another two feet above that by the perennial favorite, barbed wire.

The wire would be electrified when the gates were closed, to make the contact, Rourke surmised.

And the gates stayed closed now as the guard sergeant approached the staff ATV, saluting as Paul lowered the window and Michael produced the orders.

The sergeant said not a word, merely inspecting the orders. Natalia rolled down her window and flicked ashes from her cigarette toward the ground, beginning to speak to Rourke, as though picking up a conversation in midstream. "I disagree that the Germans have any sort of chance against us, Comrade."

John Rourke lit a cigarette—Soviet officers never smoked cigars in public, because it was still considered a capitalist affectation—and exhaled smoke as he told her, "Yes, Comrade Major, but as much as I agree and believe in the superiority of our forces, the fact remains that the German war machine, augmented as it is by the Americans and the other allies, is too strong to be ignored."

Natalia laughed, saying, "But too weak to be a threat?"

The guard sergeant cleared his throat, Natalia looking at him, saying, "Yes?"

"Comrade Major, it is necessary to see—"

"—papers," Natalia preempted, reaching into her purse and shoving the ID toward him through the open window. "We are in a great hurry." She looked away, snapping her cigarette out the window toward the guard sergeant's feet.

Rourke handed across his papers, as did Michael and Paul.

Michael cleared his throat, in what John Rourke knew was his son's best Russian, saying, "Be quick about this, Sergeant, or there will difficulties." Michael didn't explain what the difficulties might be, but the already slightly nervous-looking guard sergeant's eyes widened a little as he returned Natalia's papers. "Thank you, Comrade Major." He saluted as he spoke.

Then the guard sergeant passed back John Rourke's papers, beginning the same short speech, but Rourke waving a hand toward him, dismissing him as he continued speaking with Natalia. "You may be right that I have expressed too much caution, Comrade, but to be cautious is better than to be reckless."

"I grant you that, Comrade," Natalia smiled.

Michael's and Paul's papers were returned, and as the guard sergeant began to salute again and the deflection barricade began to lower, Paul began to drive. John Rourke released his grip on the Smith & Wesson Centennial inside the pocket of his great coat — five for sure. . . .

An ice-edged wind blew across the parade ground fronting the airfield at Gur'yev, the ice field extending in all directions as far as John Rourke could see. Far to the west was the Ural River, all but a centralmost channel ice-encrusted.

As Rourke exhaled, his breath turned to steam. He helped Natalia from the car.

"Boy, is it cold," Paul murmured, stepping back as Natalia exited the vehicle.

"Try bare legs except for these miserable nylons," Natalia told him.

Michael stepped out, all four of them walking toward the front of the staff ATV. Warmth radiated from the engine that was still running, rising in visible waves off the low armor-plated hood.

John Rourke stared toward the gate leading onto the field. Security here was less in evidence, but it was a given that the base would be on full alert after the debacle the Soviets had suffered in New Germany.

A few yards from the entrance to the field was posted a sign, the notice reading, "Only Service Vehicles Beyond This

Point."

There was a low fence of seemingly ordinary chain link, high-strength synthetic most likely, surrounding the field. Beyond this fence, and beyond the snowdrifts and massive chunks of upthrusting ice, were the runways. To the west, nearer to the river side, were the hangars, a tower, and the administrative buildings, all of these prefabricated structures and all of seemingly considerable size.

John Rourke pulled the synthetic fur officer's cap from his head, ran the bare fingers of his right hand back through his hair, and replaced the hat. He re-gloved as he spoke. "Those cars on the other side of the deflection barrier past the guard post are evidently to take visiting personnel to their destinations, then return them to the parking area. That obviates allowing any potentially large amounts of explosives onto the field."

"I'd thought you were overestimating the difficulty level," Michael observed.

"If you noticed — I did — when we parked before the inner guard post by the main entrance," Natalia said, "there was a pressure plate under us. Likely the car was scanned for explosives."

"Our guns, too?" Paul asked her.

"No. The machine wouldn't be sensitive to firearms or sensitive enough to detect explosives carried on our persons; otherwise, it would register an alarm every time a vehicle passed. If we'd had explosive loaded in the ATV, we would have betrayed ourselves."

John Rourke cupped his hands and lit another cigarette, using his Zippo this time rather than the Soviet battery-operated lighter he'd used in the car, its blue-yellow flame moving with the wind. As he snapped the cowling closed and exhaled smoke through his nostrils, he said, "I think we'd better get about our business. Remember, no guns until the last possible second. And if it's a shooting situation, let's try our best for Natalia to handle it with her suppressed weapon or for me to do it with mine, right? Let's go."

Natalia fell in at John Rourke's right side, Paul at Michael's right side, and they started toward the airfield gates in twos.

The guards evidently noticed them — three officers and a senior noncom drew themselves to attention, and the guard sergeant made a rifle salute. "Comrade Major!"

John Rourke returned the salute, saying, "Sergeant, we will require transportation to the main hangar area at once." With that, Rourke handed over his identity papers, adding to Paul Rubenstein, "Sergeant Kerensky, the orders."

"Yes, Comrade Major!" Paul offered the guard sergeant the orders, the man taking them, already returning John Rourke's identity papers. Natalia and Michael had their papers ready, Paul getting his.

"Forgive me, Comrade Major, but there is heightened security now and I must confirm these orders with Captain Michailovitch, who is the officer of the guard."

As John Rourke had suspected, the ordinary Soviet soldier had not been informed of the debacle in New Germany, or else the guard sergeant's remarks would have at least hinted at the reason.

"Very well, Sergeant," John Rourke told him. "But see to it at once." John Rourke caught the look of trepidation in his son's eyes. He turned away from his son to Natalia. "Comrade, while we wait here, allow me to inspect once again that curious object we discussed a moment ago."

Natalia smiled up at him, and her lips came together briefly as though blowing him a kiss. She opened her purse as John Rourke reached into the reinforced interior pocket of his great-coat.

Natalia's suppressor-fitted Walther PPK/S came from her shoulder bag at the same moment Rourke drew the suppressor-fitted Smith & Wesson 6906.

There were four men, John Rourke's first double tap into the neck and left eyeball of the guard sergeant as the man started to return Michael's papers. Natalia fired twice into the head of a corporal, Rourke taking out the private reaching for the guard booth radio telephone with two shots, one into the right side of the neck, the other into the right temple. Then Natalia put two bullets into the head of the last man, one through the left cheek and up into the eyeball, the second directly over the bridge of the nose.

Paul had swung back his greatcoat, his right hand going to the pistol grip of the Schmiesser submachine gun slung beneath his armpit as Michael, bare-handed, raced toward the guard booth, to operate the gate controls, Rourke knew.

"Too bad," Natalia said, not dismissively but sincerely. "Killing these men, however necessary, was a waste."

"Agreed," John Rourke nodded, grabbing one of the dead men by the heels while Natalia grabbed another, Paul working on a third. The gate was beginning to open, Michael already packing the fourth man into the guard booth.

Chapter Forty-seven

The car—something akin to a more civilized form of tracked Arctic Cat—was easy to start but cold as a tomb inside. Paul and Michael had disabled the other three identical vehicles before leaving the airfield main gate guard station.

As they drove along the perimeter of the airfield now, Paul at the wheel, John Rourke surveyed the field before them while, without thinking about the task consciously, replacing the four spent 115-grain jacketed hollow points in the magazine of the 6906.

"We should have no more than ten minutes," Natalia advised, "and more likely considerably less than that until the dead men at the gate are discovered."

"Agreed," Rourke nodded, his eyes focusing on the largest, tallest of the two hangars. Helicopters took up more room than fighter aircraft, and intelligence overflights made by the Germans confirmed Rourke's visual observations. "That largest hangar, over there, should contain the helicopter gunships, plus some sort of fuel supply for them, the main fuel dumps sensibly enough behind us, to the east." He gestured out the window, in the direction of the guard station. "The other hangar will contain fighter bombers. Michael?"

"Dad?"

"Get into the tower facility and kill everyone there, and then disable every piece of equipment you can find." John Rourke handed his son the silenced 6906. "You have five pounds of German plastique on you. Break off half and give it to Natalia. You won't need it all for the tower job."

"Right."

"Paul?"

"John?"

"You take the hangar with the fighter bombers. Get in and

plant your plastique and get out. Meet Michael near the tower, then get to the vehicle here and drive to those bunkers over there. See them?"

There were anti-aircraft troops' bunkers built to the far southern edge of the airfield. "Then what?"

"Sandbag yourselves in and wait for reinforcements. But before that, Michael, when you are about to enter the tower, and Paul, as you're about to enter the fighter bomber hangar," Rourke continued, handing Michael the two spare magazines for the 6906, "activate the signals on your wristwatches to call in the J7-V drone. That should lend enough confusion to the situation to mask your escapes and help us do the same. Then the paratroopers come and German air power, and everything's rosy."

Paul laughed under his breath. "Somehow—but, then again, maybe I'm just becoming a pessimist."

Rourke leaned forward, clapping the younger man on the shoulder. "Maybe you are," John Rourke told his friend. . . .

Natalia Anastasia Tiemerovna walked beside John Rourke listening to the click of her heels against the synthetic concrete slab that paved the prefab hangar's floor. As she walked, she opened the buttons of her greatcoat. John's coat was already open, his right hand inside the outer pocket.

The hangar was enormous. In staggered ranks of four, files twenty-five deep or better, there were fully equipped, apparently battle-ready Soviet gunships in greater abundance than she had ever seen before.

She wished, suddenly, that they could have brought with them at least one of the new energy weapons, because the helicopters were clearly so equipped. But, except for what they could carry on their bodies, the risks of detection were too great, and the energy weapons were too large and unwieldy for body carry. A day would come, she knew, when these energy weapons would be as portable and concealable as the handguns she wore in the specially tailored pockets of her greatcoat. But that was not a day to which she particularly looked forward.

Several officers, in black battle dress utilities, were standing around a large synth-fuel stove and talking. John started walking toward them.

It would start here, Natalia knew, because the hangar was too open to plant seven and one-half pounds of explosives in several different locations without being spotted, then just leave.

She began pretending to fumble in her purse, so she could reach the Walther quickly enough.

As they approached the Elite Corps officers, one of them — a woman — noticed the two senior officers approaching and called the group to attention.

John told them, "As you were, Comrades. What an excellent facility!"

The senior officer, a captain who looked to be in his late twenties, responded, "Thank you, Comrade Major. We are proud of our humble part in the defense of the Soviet."

"As well you should be, as well you should be," John nodded, smiling.

The female officer was staring at John. And what was in her eyes was clearly lust. As the woman's eyes left Rourke's for a moment and locked with Natalia's, Natalia smiled. The woman looked away, back at John, her eyes all but undressing him.

The captain cleared his throat, asking, "How might we assist you, Comrade Major?"

"Ahh, you might assist us, indeed. In light of recent events in the battle against the new imperialism, it has come to the attention of the premier — whose office I have but recently left — that there is the increased possibility of sabotage by Allied agents against the Soviet people. The Comrade Major who accompanies me" — and John gestured toward Natalia — "is an expert in such matters. If you might indicate to her quickly where the three most likely places would be that enemy agents might plant explosives in order to perpetrate the greatest harm to this facility, our work here would be vastly easier, Comrades."

"Certainly, Comrade Major. But, may I ask, three locations? Why?"

And John lit a cigarette—for an instant she thought he'd use his American-made Zippo, but he did not—leaned forward toward the captain and, in a tone that was almost conspiratorial, certainly confidential, told him, "We know for a fact, Comrade, that a group of Allied agents is active in this immediate vicinity even as we speak. We even know the amount and type of explosives they carry. The explosives are German plastique, in the quantity of slightly over fifteen kilograms."

"Comrade Major! Should that quantity of explosives be used against this facility, it could wreak almost total destruction."

As John exhaled, he told the captain, "That is most certainly their intention, Comrade, preparatory to an assault on this entire facility. The three most potentially damaging locations, if you would, Comrade, as quickly as possible, since there is not a moment to lose. And, since I have taken you into our confidence, disclosing the amount of explosives to be used, it might further facilitate our work if you might suggest to the Comrade Major how the fifteen kilograms might best be employed as concerns their most effective use."

"Yes, Comrade Major!" There was such a tone of gravity to the young captain's voice that Natalia almost felt ashamed of John for taking advantage of him so. Almost. The captain turned to her and bowed slightly, saying, "Comrade Major, if you would accompany me."

"Thank you, Comrade."

The other officers fell in a few steps behind them as the captain took them across the hangar, between two of the ranks of gunships, and toward a doorway. The sign on the door indicated that explosives were stored on the other side. "Tell me, Comrade, what type of explosives are there here and in what condition are they stored?"

"Missiles, Comrade Major, for use with our gunships in combat."

"I see. And are they armed?"

"Ohh, certainly not, Comrade, but to facilitate their replacement when many sorties must be flown in rapid succession, the detonators are stored in the same room."

"Highly susceptible to sabotage," Natalia nodded. "You have done well to show this to me. Would you say that the fuel storage area on the opposite side of the hangar is another likely spot for these saboteurs to plant their explosives? And she gestured gracefully toward the opposite end of the building, beyond where the officers had originally stood.

"Indeed, Comrade Major, if I may be so bold," he smiled, his eyes very pretty, very dark, "I have studied the use of explosives in my off hours, and were I one of these Allied saboteurs, I would merely divide the fifteen kilograms, five kilograms here and ten there, by the fuel. The resultant explosions would wash the entire structure in flaming synth fuel and collapse the main support walls, destroying everything and everyone inside."

She looked at John as he spoke. "I believe that is all we need to know, Comrade." And his left hand started moving toward the buttons of the uniform blouse he wore beneath his greatcoat.

Natalia looked at the young captain, asking him pointedly, "Comrade, I wish your most honest answer to this next question."

"Yes, Comrade Major?"

"If you were given the opportunity to save your own life while your comrades died, would you take it?"

He looked positively hurt and Natalia felt very sorry for the sincere young man. "Comrade Major! I assure you that I would never—"

She smiled her best smile, as her right hand came out of her purse, her fingers closed around the butt of the Walther. "You are a true credit to the officer corps of the Soviet Union and I am sure, someday, would have earned with great honor the Order of Lenin."

Then she shot him cleanly where the bridge of his nose met his forehead, so the bullet would penetrate the brain immediately and he would die instantly, painlessly.

As she wheeled round, there was a loud crack, but oddly muffled-sounding, as John's right hand swung up still inside the greatcoat pocket and he fired his little enclosed hammer revolver into the throat of the officer nearest to him, turning left a little and firing again, killing another of the men with a bullet to the chest. His left hand was already drawing one of the full-sized Detonics Scoremasters from under his uniform blouse. He thumbed back the hammer and shot a third officer in the head at point-blank range as the muzzle of Natalia's suppressor-fitted PPK/S swung onto the forehead of the sole female officer.

There was a pistol in the woman's hand, pointed at the back of John Rourke's head.

Natalia fired first, killing her.

John had a ScoreMaster in each hand now, firing the gleaming stainless steel .45's into the remaining officers, putting them down.

Natalia put a second round into the head of one of the men who wasn't yet dead.

As he changed magazines in his pistols, John told her, "Plant those explosives."

Chapter Forty-eight

John Rourke walked across the hangar floor, a ScoreMaster in each hand, eight-round Detonics extension magazines in the two .45's, a total of nine 185-grain jacketed hollow points per pistol.

He looked back once and saw Natalia, on her knees, her suppressor-fitted Walther beside her, just inside the doorway of the shelter in which the missiles for the gunships were stored. He'd watched as she shot out the lock. She was setting the first of the two explosive charges now.

In the distance, in this few seconds' lull before the shooting started, he could hear the sound of the drone J7-V coming in across the airfield to strike. With any luck, Aldridge would already be ashore, having knocked out the battery there, and the second battery would have been taken care of by Otto Hammerschmidt.

And Paul and Michael would be nearly through with their demolitions work.

A senior sergeant with an assault rifle in his hands ran toward John Rourke from the far side of the hangar. "What has happened, Comrade Major?"

"Saboteurs, Sergeant." John Rourke shot the man in the chest and again in the head, then walked on.

Men were streaming toward him from the rear of the hangar, armed with pistols and crowbars and large wrenches. As the first wave of them neared, John Rourke raised both ScoreMasters to shoulder level and began firing. He shot a man holding a pistol, sending the body spinning back into two other men. He shot another Elite Corpsman with a pistol. In Russian, John Rourke shouted toward two men charging toward him with nothing more than crowbars. "Turn back or I will shoot!"

They did not turn back, nor had Rourke expected them to do so. He fired, killing both men almost simultaneously.

There was gunfire from behind him, rippling across the synthetic concrete slab, some stray bullets ricocheting into the chin bubble of one of the helicopter gunships.

John Rourke turned around, firing both pistols in tandem, knocking down and killing the man firing at him.

John Rourke turned back toward the wave of angry, indifferently armed workmen. As one of them fired a pistol and missed — the range was too great for most men with a handgun — John Rourke began to systematically empty both ScoreMasters, putting down four more of the men before they turned back, withdrawing to cover.

The ScoreMasters empty, John Rourke stabbed them into the trouser band of his uniform pants, their slides still locked open over the spent magazines. He drew from first the right, then the left of the two holsters on the Alessi rig under his armpits, the twin stainless Detonics Combatmasters filling his hands, thumbs jacking back the hammers. This time, each pistol was loaded with seven rounds. His fingers flexed around the worn black checkered rubber Pachmayr grips.

From his left, a man charged toward him with a large wrench, shouting in Russian, "You will die, saboteur!"

The pistol in John Rourke's left hand fired once.

The man fell down dead.

Out of the far right corner of his peripheral vision, John Rourke could see Natalia, running across the width of the hangar toward the fuel storage area. He was about to shoot a man coming up on her with a pistol, but Natalia shot and killed him first.

John Rourke continued walking, toward the leading rank of Soviet gunships. Two men charged toward him, one firing a handgun, the other with a wrench in each hand. John Rourke fired on both men, putting them down.

The killing would stop soon, one way or the other, Rourke told himself.

He kept walking, the pistol from his right hand going into his waistband for a moment, cocked and locked. He took advantage of the momentary lull, buttoned and then pulled the

216

empty magazine from one of the ScoreMasters, and replaced it with a fresh eight-rounder. He redrew the little Combat Master, fired into the face of a man racing toward him with a crowbar, and killed him.

Rourke performed the same operation for the second ScoreMaster, redrew the second Combatmaster. He was nearing the forwardmost rank of gunships.

Two men charged him, both of them firing handguns, a bullet tearing through the skirt of Rourke's greatcoat. He emptied both Detonics miniguns into the men, then stuffed the pistols, slides locked open, into his waistband, drawing the two ScoreMasters. His right thumb swept down the slide release, the slide of the pistol in his right hand snapping forward, stripping and chambering the top round out of the magazine.

He turned the second ScoreMaster in his left hand, bringing his left thumb around to the left side of the pistol, dropping the slide stop, then regripping the pistol properly.

Rourke walked along the forwardmost rank of gunships.

An Elite Corpsman with a pistol stepped out, Rourke dodging right as the man fired, the Elite Corpsman's bullet missing. But Rourke fired both ScoreMasters simultaneously. And he didn't miss.

There were explosions outside now, a heavy volume of machine gun fire, but no sounds of anti-aircraft batteries opening up on the drone.

John Rourke safed both ScoreMasters as he climbed up into one of the gunships, thumbs poised over the safeties as he walked forward, ducking under the overhead.

The gunship was empty.

As he sat down in the cockpit, the pistols going between his legs, muzzles against the seat surface, his fingers began activating electrical systems. His eyes moved over the floor of the hangar. Natalia was almost finished, it seemed, near the fuel storage area.

Rourke's eyes moved to the instrument panel.

All systems on, fuel gauges registering full.

He started the main rotor.

The engine turned over instantly.

217

Oil pressure was already beginning to build as he flipped the switch for the tail rotor.

Natalia was coming away from the fuel storage area now, looking for him.

John Rourke climbed out of the cockpit, guns in hand again, and went to the fuselage doorway on the starboard side. "Natalia! Here. Change in plans!"

She waved to him and began to run, looking slightly ridiculous in high heels and a skirt with a revolver in each hand.

John Rourke checked to port and starboard of the gunship. If men still lived inside here, they were holding back.

He went forward, dropping down into the pilot's seat again. Nearly full pressure.

Nearly sufficient RPMs.

Through the hangar doors, he could see activity on the airfield outside, moving vehicles, running men, an explosion.

He heard Natalia's voice behind him. "Anything I need to do?"

"I don't think we're lashed down, but double-check," Rourke called back.

While he waited, he reloaded both Detonics miniguns, holstering the pistols under his arms, then lowering the hammers of the two ScoreMasters, replacing the pistols into his trouser band.

Again, from behind him, came Natalia's voice. "We have about two minutes until—"

"I know. Strap in, Natalia," Rourke told her.

She took the seat beside him. He enjoyed having Natalia beside him, like few other sensations in his life.

John Rourke increased rotation, starting to lift off ever so slightly.

"I hate this," Natalia said. "Flying inside a building."

John Rourke said nothing, very gently altering rotor pitch, the gunship starting to edge forward over the floor. At last, he told her, "Check that our weapons systems are all operational and give me machine guns."

"Right. About ninety seconds, John, and the whole building goes."

"Right," Rourke nodded.

218

Men were running into the hangar through the large doors. Had this been some sort of spy thriller from five centuries ago, they would have immediately apprehended what was happening and begun to close the hangar doors, to block the helicopter's exit.

But it wasn't and they didn't.

Instead, about a dozen men took up positions behind parts, crates, and other gunships, shouldering their assault rifles. "We have machine guns up, Natalia?"

"Yes."

John Rourke nodded. He flipped his control switches, activating forward firing port and starboard guns dead on toward the riflemen now beginning to fire at him, the heavier rounds of the machine guns fired with such rapidity that a burst seemed like one long shot tore through the packing crates, spilling the men sheltered behind them to the concrete slab. Rourke maneuvered his machine slightly to port, angling the forward firing guns still more, firing toward the men in cover among the choppers.

"Missiles up?"

"Yes. We have forty-three seconds, John."

"Right." John Rourke let the gunship turn ninety degrees on the axis of the main rotor, activating a single starboard side missile, rotating away from it and increasing speed as the contrail vanished among the gunships still ranked in the hangar.

The explosion from the missile rocked the building's walls, a fireball belching after them as Rourke looked back once and increased speed to escape it.

He was only a few feet below the roof supports now, and too near the ground for comfort still. "When we get outside, look for Paul and for Michael. If we can pick them up, they'll be safer."

"All right. Twenty-one seconds, John."

Rourke only nodded, increasing speed gradually, almost to the doors.

Men ran through the open doorway, firing assault rifles, Rourke firing the gunship's port and starboard forward machine guns, getting most of them.

As he flew past, there was a blur at the far left corner of his peripheral vision. "Natalia! Port side fuselage door."

"All right."

As he glanced toward Natalia, he saw her leveling the suppressor-fitted PPK/S, firing it once, then again and again. He looked back and down through the chin bubble, saw the body rolling beneath them.

"Eight seconds, John."

Rourke nodded, nearly into the open.

Automatic weapons fire tore across the chin bubble but didn't penetrate. Rourke veered away from it, catching sight of three men with assault rifles to his far left.

"Four seconds. Three. Two, now. One."

John Rourke gunned the main rotor, the gunship dipping, slipping right in the sudden draft, Rourke radically altering main rotor pitch, the gunship escaping the open hangar doors as the explosions came from behind him, occurring almost simultaneously.

Rourke started the gunship climbing, let it rotate one hundred eighty degrees, and looked back. Secondary and tertiary explosions were ripping through the hangar structure now, the walls of the immense prefab building bulging outward, then collapsing inward as the roof fell and fireballs rushed upward into the freezing air.

"I see Michael."

Rourke looked to his left, banked the chopper to port, and started to descend, skimming over the runway now. He saw Paul, just ahead of Michael, both of them running toward the bunkers at the far end of the field.

There was an explosion from the control tower, then another, the tower teetering like a chopped-through tree, swaying, the legs collapsing under it, the structure falling forward into the airfield, another explosion coming.

To Rourke's right, the roof of the smaller hangar — the one for the fighter bombers — seemed to ripple front to back, and then a fireball tore through its center, belching skyward in the hot updraft.

Gunfire tore across the surface of the field, near to Michael, too near.

Rourke let the machine rotate ninety degrees to port and

220

began to climb, the source of the gunfire a vehicle with a machine gun mounted to its rear end. Rourke almost whispered, "Activating one starboard missile now." He fired, then turned away from the contrail, back toward Michael and Paul.

The two men were even with one another now, Michael always a faster runner than Paul, but both of them swapping gunfire with riflemen from the far end of the field, neither Paul's submachine gun nor Michael's pistols adequate for the distance involved. Rourke banked the gunship, brought it ninety degrees to starboard, and fired a pair of missiles toward the riflemen, banking to port, easing downward toward the surface of the field.

Rourke looked behind him. In the distance, J7-Vs were approaching from the west, over the Ural River. And, as he looked forward again, Natalia said, "There, John! The Germans!"

German gunships were moving in from the east, coming low over the field, missiles and guns firing. "Natalia—"

"I'm already changing frequencies, John." She switched into German from English. "This is Soviet gunship KH R 333 658, piloted by John Rourke. This is Major Tiemerovna speaking. We are moving directly toward German helicopter force, flying east over center of field to pick up Michael Rourke and Paul Rubenstein. Hold your fire against us. I repeat, this is Major Tiemerovna, in gunship—"

He nearly had them. Michael and Paul were starting to run toward them, to intercept their line of flight.

At the far left corner of Rourke's peripheral vision, he saw a moving vehicle, one of the Soviet energy weapons mounted to it. "Shit," John Rourke almost whispered.

He banked to port, taking elevation, the energy weapon firing, a ripple of white-hot lightning coming from its muzzle, Rourke banking to starboard, the energy beam flickering beneath the chin bubble.

Rourke banked the machine to port and started a dive, activating forward firing port and starboard missiles for full battery shots.

As the energy weapon fired upward at them, Rourke fired, forward firing missile batteries launching from port and starboard, the contrails vanishing toward the vehicle firing on the gunship as Rourke banked.

The gunship vibrated and the control panels died. "What was that?"

"Energy weapon strike," Rourke answered, flicking switches, then reaching to the overhead, going to auxiliary power as he looked to port.

The vehicle with the energy weapon was lost within a fireball—black and orange and yellow—of tremendous size. The gunship was going down. "John?"

"We're not dead yet," John Rourke shouted to her, the wind rush around the cockpit growing to maddening intensity, the gunship starting to spin.

He tried auxiliary power again.

Nothing.

"Intruder defense."

"What?"

"Intruder defense," Rourke repeated, hitting the system activation switch. Soviet gunships were equipped with an intruder defense system that discharged a high voltage electrical current through the skin. "Don't touch anything at all!" Electricity arced around them as the gunship spiraled downward, the pressure against Rourke's kidneys, in his throat. . . . The charge dissipated, the ground rushing upward.

John Rourke hit the emergency power switch again.

His instrument panel pulsed, died, pulsed, and he had power.

John Rourke gave full power to the tail rotor, edging power into the main rotor's engine.

The gunship stabilized, Rourke advancing power on the main rotor, the gunship slipping left, Rourke skimming it over the airfield.

Toward Michael and Paul.

Almost, he thought, almost verbalizing it.

"Lower, John," Natalia told him.

And John Rourke smiled, thinking about the old jokes from five centuries ago about women being backseat drivers.

"John?"

"Coming in," he told her, slipping the machine to starboard, cutting back on main rotor power, pitching downward, then gliding to a landing.

Paul and Michael ran toward the ship, Michael vaulting inside as John Rourke looked back, then Paul diving in after him, shouting, "Take her up!"

John Rourke changed pitch and added power, the gunship arcing upward, Rourke rotating it a full three hundred sixty degrees, then giving full power to the main rotor as he banked to port, toward the German gunship force. "John. They see us, are telling us to climb. Both the shore and inland batteries are destroyed with minimal casualties. We have them. We have them! I could kiss you!"

John Rourke looked at Natalia Tiemerovna.

As he started the gunship climbing, he found one of the thin, dark tobacco cigars from inside his uniform blouse, then clamped it tightly between his teeth.

Another skirmish won, the final battle just ahead.